"HEAVENS, WHAT WOULD MY GIRLS BE DOING HERE AT THIS HOUR?"

"I came to see if you were comfortable," a she-male voice went on.

"Mrs. Bordon?" asked Longarm.

"Call me Livia," she replied, sliding under the covers with him. As their hips touched, he could tell she wasn't wearing a thin nightgown. She was bare-ass naked!

Longarm said, "Well, far be it from me to refuse kind hospitality, ma'am. But are you sure your husband won't mind...?"

TABOR EVANS

LONGARM

ON THE
GREAT DIVIDE

A JOVE BOOK

LONGARM ON THE GREAT DIVIDE

A Jove Book / published by arrangement with
the author

PRINTING HISTORY
Jove edition / February 1983

ISBN: 0-515-06253-7

Jove books are published by Jove Publications, Inc.,
200 Madison Avenue, New York, N. Y. 10016. The words
"A JOVE BOOK" and the "J" with sunburst are trademarks
belonging to Jove Publications, Inc.

Chapter 1

Saturday morning in Denver smelled just awful down by the Burlington Yards. But Longarm hadn't headed that way because he admired the smells of coal smoke and cow. Henry's Saloon, between the stock pens and the Union Station, was about the only inexpensive drinking establishment a man might find open at such a grim gray hour. The office wouldn't open for another hour or more, and meanwhile a man had to stay awake.

Longarm hadn't risen early. He'd been up all night, and he was mad as hell about it. He'd wasted the better part of Friday night on an Eastern tourist gal who'd said she wanted to see the sights of Denver and thanked Longarm for a lovely evening with a handshake in the lobby of her infernal hotel. Then he'd gone to the Black Cat to see if the new she-male barkeep there needed someone to walk her home safe after she got off at three, and damned if she hadn't found herself a steady man already. The son of a bitch might have had the decency to show up early instead of waiting about outside for the sassy flirt. But, what the hell, some Friday nights were like that, and the office only stayed open until noon on Saturday. So Longarm figured he'd kill the leftover time talking cow with the good old boys at Henry's

1

and then surprise Marshal Billy Vail by showing up at the office on time.

Henry's was a hole in the wall, laid out like the Longbranch in Dodge, with the bar running the length of the narrow space. As Longarm strode through the swinging doors, he saw that the place was almost deserted. Old Henry's son-in-law, Zeke, sat behind the bar reading *Ned Buntline's True Tales of the Wild West,* with a mounted buffalo head on the wall seeming to read over his shoulder. Down at the far end, a middle-aged, well-dressed gent was nursing a bottle of Kentucky. He had a leather bag like lawyers carried on the bar in front of him. Longarm enjoyed talking cow, now that he didn't have to herd the infernal beasts any longer, but he heard all the law talk he wanted to, working as a deputy marshal for the Justice Department. So he bellied up near Zeke and ordered a schooner of draft. As tired as he was, he knew better than to drink anything stronger at this hour.

Longarm was halfway down the beer schooner and debating whether or not to wander on to a more exciting part of town when two Denver lawmen he knew came in. One was a detective named Sullivan and the other a uniformed copper badge named Doyle. They nodded to Longarm but kept going. He watched with interest as they joined the quiet stranger down at the far end.

The stranger seemed surprised, too. Sullivan asked him if he was Mr. Skean, who owned the hardware business on Larimer Street, and when the man allowed he was, Sullivan said, "Your wife said we might find you here, sir. We called first at your home. She said you told her you had to meet a business associate down here."

Skean nodded. "She told you true. I'm waiting for the morning train from Pueblo. What can I do for you boys?"

Sullivan took out his notebook and a pencil stub. "I fear we have bad news for you, sir," he said. "Your business partner, Milton Gross, was murdered about three o'clock this morning. It looks as though he walked in on a burglar."

Skean's jaw dropped and his face went ashen. Then he

pulled himself together and managed to say, "Oh, my God, that's awful! But how could it have happened? What could old Milt have wanted at our store at three o'clock in the morning?"

Sullivan nodded. "That's likely what the burglar or burglars counted on. They had the safe open when your partner walked in on them, whatever his reason. Nobody heard the shots, but one of our roundsmen noticed the front door was unlocked when he come down Larimer. Your partner was inside on the floor full of lead. The coroner's examining the body. What can you tell us about the contents of the safe?"

"I can't give you the exact figures," the merchant replied with a frown. "Milt was running the store yesterday afternoon while I was out on business. But there must have been a pretty penny. You see, the banks close at three and we stay open late on Friday evening, so the receipts spend the weekend in the safe. I'd have to go over Milt's stubs to give you the exact figure."

"Round guesses will do for now, Mr. Skean."

Skean shrugged. "I just don't know. We seldom do more than a hundred dollars' worth of business on any given day, but . . . Oh, Lord, I nearly forgot! We're expecting a C.O.D. on some barbed wire and a Sunflower windmill we ordered for a customer. If Milt took the cash from the bank to pay for the C.O.D. yesterday afternoon, there'd have been over a thousand in that safe."

Longarm found himself getting interested. He picked up his drink and drifted down to join them, asking, "When was your customer supposed to take delivery—and, more important, when were you gents expecting that hardware to arrive?"

Skean eyed him warily.

"It's all right, he's law, too," Sullivan said.

So Skean replied, "The shipment was due in Monday morning. We get a discount for cash, so Milt would have wanted it handy in case it showed up before the banks open at nine. But never mind about the damn money! What are

3

you doing about catching my partner's killer?"

Sullivan started to soothe Skean. Longarm finished his beer, put the schooner on the bar, and said, "Fill that up again, Zeke. We've already caught the killer, Skean."

Everyone in the place stared blankly at Longarm. He shook his head wearily and said to Sullivan, "What are you pussyfooting around for? Don't you aim to *arrest* this son of a bitch?"

Sullivan and his associate were still looking blank as Skean crawfished away from the bar, going for the S&W .38 under his frock coat. Longarm had figured he might, so he'd palmed his own .44 derringer before joining the conversation. As Skean's muzzle cleared leather, Longarm fired both barrels of his small but deadly derringer.

Skean slammed into the wall and slid down it to come to rest in a seated position on the floor, dead as anyone would be with two rounds of .44 in his heart.

As the smoke cleared, Longarm saw that the other two lawmen had their own guns out. He broke open his derringer to reload it as he observed mildly, "You boys surely move slow for the line of work you're in. Zeke, I reckon we'd best have three more drinks down here. I ain't buying for the rascal on the floor."

"Damn it, Longarm, we've asked you not to gun customers in here," Zeke said. "You promised to cut it out after you winged Soapy Smith in here that time."

Longarm didn't reply. Sullivan stared in wonder at the cadaver sitting on the floor as he put his own gun away, saying, "Well, slapping leather on three growed lawmen sort of constitutes a confession. But how in hell did you know, Longarm?"

"He told me. Told you, too, if you'd been paying any attention. You ain't awake yet, Sullivan. Let's have us a morning bracer and then you'll likely find that the bullets from that rascal's gun match up with the ones in his partner's body. Meanwhile, let's have a peek in this here bag."

Longarm opened the bag and spilled the contents on the bar.

4

Sullivan whistled. "There must be *more'n* a thousand dollars there!"

Longarm nodded. "I figured as much. Can you see what happened now, or do I have to draw you a picture?"

Sullivan hefted one of the wads of paper money and shook his head. "Nope. Anyone can see what must have happened. Skean was fixing to cut out on his wife and partner for whatever reason. So he was helping hisself to their mutual funds when the partner walked in on him. The late Milton Gross must have been suspicious, or maybe he was just passing the hardware store and wondered why it was open at such an ungodly hour. Anyway, Gross found Skean in the safe, asked why, and got answered with six rounds of .38. We already had the caliber figured, and this money proves the rest of the sad familiar tale. But let's back up a mite, Longarm. You said he *told* you all this? Where the hell was I when Skean was doing all this confessing?"

"Standing right there with your fool notebook. When you boys came in and told him his partner had been shot, you never said where he'd been shot. You said he'd walked in on a burglary, period. Skean, not you, started talking about the hardware store. Study that, Sullivan. The store was closed for the weekend. How did Skean know Gross didn't surprise a burglar in his own home, where he should have been at three o'clock on a Saturday morning?"

"By God, you're right! I missed that entire."

"You missed something else. Didn't it strike you as odd that a man who'd had a burglary surprised in his own store never asked if any money had been taken?"

Doyle snapped his fingers and said, "Damn! That *is* the first question folks always ask when we tell 'em they've had a burglary! The rascal didn't ask if there was anything left in his safe because he knew damned well it was in that there bag!"

By this time, the grumpy Zeke had placed three drinks on the bar by the bag. Longarm picked his up and said, "I can see you boys are fully awake now. Would you do me a favor, Sullivan?"

"Christ, yes! I suspicion I owe you our lives as well as a mighty sudden solution to a tedious mystery. What's your pleasure, old son?"

"I got to get on up to the federal building in time to go to work. Why don't you boys just leave me out of your report and save me the damned coroner's hearing?"

Sullivan frowned. "Don't you want credit for solving the crime, Longarm?" he asked.

"Hell, I solve crimes all the time," Longarm said. "The paperwork is a bitch. What this rascal done was local, not federal. So I'd be obliged if you locals took full credit and just let me read about it in the papers."

Sullivan looked at his associate, who nodded, grinning.

"That sure is neighborly of you, Longarm. We won't forget the favor," Sullivan said.

Longarm glanced at the clock on the wall and finished his drink. "Hell, boys, you don't owe me," he said. "I owe you. You just helped me pass some tedious time and I thank you for the diversion. But now, if it's all the same with you, I'd best be on my way. I can't wait to see the expression on Marshal Vail's face when he finds me waiting for him when the office opens this morning."

It didn't work out the way Longarm had planned at the office. He got to the federal building so early he had to knock on the big bronze doors and get the night watchman to let him in. But when he arrived at the second-story U. S. marshal's office he smelled the awesome reek of the cheap cigars his boss smoked. Longarm cursed softly and lit one of his own cheroots before he went on in. The reception room was deserted. Nobody but a boob or an idjet showed up an hour early on the salary Uncle Sam paid.

Longarm strode over to the door of Marshal Vail's inner sanctum and opened it, saying, "Morning, you poor idjet."

Marshal Vail looked up from the pack-rat's nest of papers on his desk. "It's about time you got here, Longarm," he said. "I got a chore for you, as soon as I can find it in this mess. I came in early to get caught up on my paperwork, but them purple-pissing sons of bitches in Washington keep sending me more infernal forms to fill out. I'd sure like to get my hands on the rascals who invented typewriting machines and carbon paper. It wasn't like this in the good old days when I was riding with the Rangers. If me and Captain Bigfoot had taken time to write out every infernal thing in triplicate, the Comanches and the Mexicans would still own Texas!"

Longarm took a seat across the desk from his older, shorter, plumper boss. "They calls it modern progress, Billy," he said. "I never had to come to work wearing this fool shoestring tie before old President Hayes and his First Lady started serving lemonade at the White House, neither. What did you have in mind for me this morning? I do so hope you recall that it's Saturday and that Lincoln freed the slaves?"

Vail fished a yellow sheet from the pile and answered, "Here she is. I'm sending you up to the Divide, near Tolland. The Post Office Department has asked Justice for a hand, and you're it."

Longarm blew a thoughtful smoke ring. "That sounds fair. But would you mind telling me what I'll be doing up in the high range, Billy?"

"Working, of course," Vail said. "The Post Office has been having trouble with an outfit called the Timberliners. Name mean anything to you?"

Longarm scowled. "You know it does. This is getting mighty tedious, Billy. I have put the late Timberline Younger in the same grave twice, and if you're saying he's up and about again, I quit!"

Vail laughed and said, "Relax. We're not jawing about an outlaw called Timberline. This here is a gang of train robbers."

"You call that an improvement? Don't tell me why they're called the Timberliners. I know the country up there is above timberline. But what in thunder are they doing robbing trains in such a godforsaken neck of the woods? I didn't know those private narrow-gaugers between the mining camps up there even carried the U. S. Mail."

Vail shrugged. "Hell, somebody has to. How else would the miners get their mail? The mail sacks they've been interfering with up in the high range don't amount to all that much. It's the silver from the mines the gang seems interested in. But while stopping the trains to rob them of silver, they've interfered with the U. S. Mail—and that's a federal crime, in case you forgot."

Longarm snorted in disgust. "I know the law. The Postal dicks know it, too. So how come we have to pull their chestnuts out of the fire, Billy? Don't the Postmaster General have any guns on his payroll these days?"

"He does, and they keep getting shot. That's where you come in. My opposing number in the Post Office Department asked for you personally. It's your own fault for solving that other mail case on the Big Muddy. The Timberliners have killed a couple of well-meaning dudes and vanished one sent by Washington. This gang is savvy to the high country and mean as hell. It's going to take someone just as mean and just as savvy to the mountains to stay alive long enough to get a line on them. How many deputies do you figure you'll need to back your play?"

Longarm blew another smoke ring before he answered. "Let's eat this apple one bite at a time, Billy. You know I work best alone. Sometimes it helps to know in advance just what I'm up against. What's the catch?"

"Catch?" Vail asked innocently.

Longarm smiled crookedly. "Don't shit me, Chief. I know you of old. I know the country up along the Divide, too, and if there was one place on earth I had to pick *not* to rob a train, narrow-gauge or wide, above timberline would be it. The sheep range up there is rough but wide open. A short man on a short horse can see fifty miles or more in every direction from any rise close enough to matter. The last I heard, they had a sheriff and such up in Gilpin County, and I doubt the miners' vigilance committees are pleased at not getting letters from home. So let's hear the spooky part. We're surely now jawing about a plain old gang of train robbers, right?"

Vail leaned back in his chair, smiled fondly at Longarm, and said, "You see? You ain't even left my office and you've already started tracking smart. That is what's got the Post Office and the railroad company feeling spooked, Longarm. You're right about its being wide-open country, and the locals up there know every one of the few possible hiding places, so they've all been checked out more'n once. The gang's method is simple. They just make 'em stop the train. Then they bust open the mail car, shooting anybody who argues about it, and help themselves to whatever they fancy."

"Sounds like a regular James-Younger holdup so far. Get to the hard part, Billy."

"They ride away with the loot. That's when it gets hard. Naturally, the train crew throws the engine in gear and reports the robbery at the next stop. Then everybody gets excited, forms a posse, and rides to the scene of the holdup. And that's it. They never find any sign to follow. The Timberliners and their loot are gone. Vamoosed. Vanished from the face of the earth."

"Hmm. Naturally, the posse circles some, looking for sign?"

"They do better than that. A pony can only carry a man and his loot so far. And there's only so many trails down from the high country, so the possemen have been wiring ahead, and trailblocks have been set up. Do I have to tell you how many desperadoes have been intercepted by these attempts?"

Longarm shook his head. "Not hardly. If the gang had ridden into one trailblock, we wouldn't be having this fool discussion. Has it come to anyone that they could just be laying low somewhere up above the timberline till the heat dies down?"

"It has, and you are right about it being possible to see mighty far amidst the peaks of the Divide. The country ain't

9

deserted totally. There are scattered sheepherders on the barren grounds, and cattle outfits along the timberline, and from there on down to everywhere there's decent footing. Nobody has ever spotted a band of mounted strangers going anywhere at all within an hour of a holdup. They can't be riding off across the sheep range, or they'd have left at least one hoofprint for some posseman to read. Before you ask about caves and abandoned mine shafts, they've been checked out, too. In the first place, there ain't all that many, and in the second, it's granite country with no natural caves, and all the mines dug by white men in this century mapped."

Longarm started to wonder aloud about the mines dug by Indians, but he knew it was too foolish a question to ask. Both the mountain Utes and Arapaho had been Stone-Age peoples who'd never mined enough to matter. Longarm took a drag on his cheroot, let the smoke out, and said, "Well, that leaves a gang mounted on flying horses, or maybe a private airship. I can't go along with flying horses, and *Scientific American* says they're a ways from perfecting the airship yet."

He blew a thoughtful smoke signal before he added, "Somebody has to be telling some fibs, Billy. It just won't work any other way."

Vail nodded. "I had that already figured out, just sitting here, old son. I doubt like hell you'll catch anyone in any lies here in our office. On the other hand, there's a train leaving for Tolland before ten, and you can make it easy."

Longarm looked wistfully at the banjo clock on the wall. "I was figuring on knocking off for the day at noon, Billy."

Vail smiled crookedly and replied, "I figured you'd been up all night. You can rest on the train, pay the usual courtesy calls on the local law up there, and be ready to start early in the morning."

"Why, Chief, tomorrow's Sunday! Are you telling me to break the Sabbath?"

"Those trains they're robbing run seven days a week, and what I want you to break is the goddamned case. Just use your rail pass on the D&RG for now and we'll work

10

out your per diem when you get back."

Longarm rose to his considerable height and turned to leave before his boss could find more work for him. But Vail couldn't resist adding, "I'm sure glad you showed up so early for a change, old son. Had you been as late as usual, you'd have missed the early train and had to catch the one this evening."

Longarm didn't reply. He walked out to the corridor, saw it was still deserted, and took off his hat to throw it down and give it a good swift kick. It didn't do either the Stetson or Longarm a bit of good. He picked up his battered hat, put it back on, and left the building cursing the dumb son of a bitch who'd written that virtue was its own reward.

Chapter 2

Longarm caught the damn train. He couldn't think of anything better to do, unless it was in bed. Longarm was in good shape and could last seventy-two hours without sleep if he had anything interesting going on about him. But the slow train ride up the eastern slope of the Rockies wasn't all that interesting even when a body was wide awake, once he'd seen it a couple of times. Longarm had lost count of the times he'd ridden the train between Denver and Salt Lake. So he didn't have to look out the grimy window to know that after a spell the rolling prairie west of Denver humped itself up into barren foothills, or that after the tracks hairpinned up a ways the short grass gave way to aspen glades and lodgepole pine at modest altitude, followed by broody dark spruce on the cooler high slopes until you reached the alpine meadows above the timberline, and so on, until a man just wanted to close his eyes.

The coach was crowded and stuffy. Longarm knew it was impolite to open a window on a train figuring to be going through a mess of tunnels while blowing soft coal smoke out of its engine stacks. There were two engine stacks because the railroad used two locomotives to haul the combination up the grade at a tedious pace. The train would make up for it by going lickety-split down the western slopes behind one engine, but Longarm would be getting off before that happy event.

Longarm had taken a coach seat near the rear of the car with his back to the bulkhead, of course. The conductor got to him last, and since they knew one another, the conductor didn't even ask to see Longarm's rail pass. He said, "Howdy, Longarm. I'll bet you're getting off at Tolland, right?"

"Lord willing and the creeks don't rise. Can I make connections to the narrow-gauge there, or do I have to look for the damn thing?"

"A little of both, Longarm. The narrow-gauge runs a spur to an ore tip alongside the trackage. But to catch their passenger combo you got to take the stage from Tolland north to Peacock City. It's a short hop. Uh, it is the Amalgamated Line you want, right?"

"Yep. Is there any other?"

"Sure, there's a more civilized mountain railroad running north at a more sensible altitude from Tolland. That one takes you through Eldora, Tungsten, Jamestown, and such. But that ain't the spur that's been getting robbed by the Timberliners."

Longarm shot him a curious look. "Who told you I was on that case, Pop? I only found out myself a few minutes ago."

The conductor smiled and explained, "A little birdie told me. To tell the truth, I heard a couple of railroad dicks jawing about it back at the depot we just left. They said it was about time the feds sent a sensible gent up to the high country to catch them rascals. One of 'em says he once saw you in action on the Missouri Pacific. His name's Hank McArtle. Do you remember him?"

Longarm frowned. "Can't connect the name to any face. Is he on this combination, Pop?"

"Nope. Working the Denver depot for pickpockets, baggage thieves, and such. We're not carrying a riding dick this trip. Those train robbers up a ways haven't been hitting the broad-gauge or, come to think of it, any of the private

13

narrow-gauges, save the Amalgamated Line."

He paused to let that sink in before he added, with a fingertip against the side of his nose, "Handcars."

Longarm frowned up at him. "Say again?"

"Handcars. It's the only way. I've passed it on to the higher-ups. They say it's my job to punch tickets and not to play detective. But, hell, a man has plenty of time to think on this infernal tedious run, and I got it all put together. The reason nobody can cut the trail of them train robbers is because they never ride away from the tracks. They got them a handcar to escape off down the same tracks on, see?"

Longarm wasn't as quick to dismiss suggestions from outsiders as some lawmen. So he studied on it as the scenery outside started moving even more slowly. They were climbing Wheat Ridge, about ten miles out of Denver. The foothills would start getting more serious in a while. Longarm said, "I follow your drift on the handcar to a point, Pop. But more than one owlhoot has used the old trick of unsaddling his mount to let it graze innocently in some pasture while escaping aboard something else, even though it's usually another horse with a different set of shoes."

The conductor chortled. "There you go. Handcars. They climb aboard some old handcar they found abandoned by one of the old bottomed-out mines up there and away they go. A handcar can go forty miles an hour or more on a favorable grade, and—"

Longarm cut in. "I said I followed you to a *point,* Pop. Your notion would explain how they got clear of the scene of the crime before any posse could get there. It would even explain why the Timberliners are concentrating on one isolated mountain railroad, since picking up a couple of tons of handcar and packing it over to some more distant tracks sounds sort of tedious. But there's a hole in your notion. Handcars run on *tracks*. Where would they keep this mysterious handcar between jobs?"

"Hell, that's easy. Same place they found it, Longarm. There's old rusty rail sidings running off the narrow-gauge main line to a dozen or more ghost mines. I say the gang is using an old ghost mine for a hideout betwixt jobs. Just mark my words and you'll see when you catch up with the sons of bitches!"

Longarm said he'd study on it and the conductor moved on. But the lawman was too sleepy right now to study on anything that complicated. A baby was crying down at the far end of the coach. He gazed out the window and swore wearily as he recognized a familiar grass-covered hog-back ridge. They were barely out of Denver, with a hundred miles or more to go, and the infernal train was crawling!

Longarm could sleep sitting up, if he felt safe. But napping in a coach seat, exposed to the world at large, wasn't a smart notion when a man had more than one old enemy at large, too. He knew there were a couple of Pullman cars up ahead and that Pop would likely let him flop in an empty compartment if he asked politely. But the trouble with a slow hundred-mile trip was that while it was too long for a tired gent to sit up, it wouldn't be long enough to do any serious sleeping.

Like most strong men, Longarm knew his few weaknesses of character. Once he found himself sound asleep on a soft Pullman bunk, it would hurt even worse to get up so soon.

He rose and strolled back to the club car, lighting a cheroot on the way. He didn't want a drink. He knew that as the train climbed to higher and thinner air, alcohol hit the brain harder, and his brain was having enough trouble staying awake as it was. Denver was already a mile above sea level, but Longarm was used to it and knew his capacity there. He'd never have had those early beers had he known that Billy Vail was sending him halfway to the damned old summer sky. The beer from Henry's was starting to repeat on him. Not enough to make him feel drunk, but enough to make him want to lie down and sleep for a million years. He ignored the crowd in the smoke-filled club car and moved out to the deserted observation platform. The mountain air tasted a whole lot better than what he'd been inhaling of late. So Longarm sat down on one of the two folding chairs, braced a booted foot up on the railing, and contemplated the railroad ties receding toward the east as he smoked and fought to keep his eyes open.

Meanwhile, far to the west, two other men were wide awake as they rode innocent-faced into the mountain town of Tolland. Tolland was little more than a hamlet clustered around the water tank and open shed depot that justified its being a settlement at all. There were fewer than two hundred people who had legal reason to reside there. So everyone in Tolland knew everyone else. On the other hand, there was enough innocent business connected with the railroad, general store, post office, and saloon to justify the occasional presence of strangers dressed cow. The nearest serious law was the county sheriff, twelve miles away in Central City. His residing deputy in Tolland was usually too busy running the general store to question strangers who weren't doing anything serious.

The older and meaner-looking of the two roughly dressed riders said, "We'd best tether our ponies in front of the post office and wait in yon saloon a spell. Longarm's train won't get here for a couple of hours, and it makes folks wonder when strangers just stand about in the open air."

His partner said, "They'll likely remember our faces, do we spend that long a time buying drinks offen them, Lynx. What if we was to just wait by the depot shed, sort of sitting and whittling?"

"Some nosy railroad gent would likely ask if we wanted tickets on the train that's comin', so *he'd* remember us, too. Remember us more serious than any barkeep. The railroad's edgy about them holdups to the north. Ain't nobody been holding up *saloons* and, in case you're blind, it's darker indoors than out on such a sunny day."

They reined in, dismounted, and tethered their mounts where Lynx had suggested. As they walked down the boardwalk toward the saloon closer to the tracks a young woman wearing a sunbonnet approached them uncertainly from the other way.

16

Lynx ticked the brim of his black sombrero and said, "Morning, ma'am," as he stepped aside respectfully to let her pass.

She didn't answer, of course. His partner muttered, "Why'd you talk to that she-male? She's sure to remember us now."

"Simmer down, Spud," Lynx said. "She was gonna remember us in any case, and she'd have done a better job had we acted uncivil. What are you so proddy about, kid? Ain't you never gunned a man before?"

"You know damn well I has," Spud growled. "But I got good reason to be proddy about the son of a bitch they sent us after this time. They say Longarm's got a cat beat when it comes to having nine lives."

"Don't worry. Betwixt us, we carry two dozen bullets in our guns. Let's have us a drink on it and steady your nerves some. Before we go in, though, do you have the form down pat?"

Spud nodded. "Sure. When his train comes in we take up stations at opposite ends of the platform. As he gets down from the coach we'll have him in a crossfire, so no matter who he's facing, the other one can gun him in the back."

"Right. If he alights facing you, don't make a move and I'll do him. If he's facing me, I'll be counting on you to hit him in the spine and not me in the face."

"They say he draws mighty fast, Lynx."

"So what? He won't slap leather at a gent who's not making any hostile moves, will he?" Lynx scoffed.

"I surely hope not, if it's me he winds up facing. Even if we get him, there's going to be hell to pay, Lynx. I don't see why the boss wants him gunned in the first place. They're bound to send another one in his place."

Lynx chuckled. "Hell, if we gun Longarm, the feds will likely send an army of deputies to take his place. But they won't know the boss on sight. Longarm does. That's why the boss wants his mission to end right here in Tolland."

• • •

Way down the tracks, Longarm's cheroot had gone out, because he was too tired to keep puffing on it. He didn't notice as he chewed the end in his teeth. He stared wearily at a familiar butte receding at a snail's pace and cursed the D&RG Western from its board of directors down to the idjets who'd laid the track at such a grade. The train rattled across a trestle crossing a little white-water stream with greener cottonwoods and alders growing along its banks. The range was breaking out in boulders and a few sizable sandstone outcroppings now. But they wouldn't really be in what serious folk called the Rocky Mountains until aspen and granite rocks showed up.

A woman in a big picture hat came out onto the platform. Longarm started to rise, politely, but she said, "Please remain seated, sir." So he did.

Damn, he was tired. He didn't even look at the gal enough to matter as she sat down across the doorway from him.

But she looked at him, laughed, and said, "Custis Long, you old hoss thief! What are you doing aboard this train?"

He turned, blinking the cobwebs from his eyes, and recognized her. "Trying to stay awake as far as Tolland, Miss Ruby," he said. "You sure are looking young and pretty, considering how long it's been since last I saw you."

It was the simple truth. Ruby LaRue—if that was her real name—had been one of the nicer-looking gals working for Madame Moustache in Dodge when he'd first come West after the War and, not knowing any better, had worked for a spell herding cows.

Longarm had never slept with her, pretty as she'd been, since he'd had a romantic nature even in his cowhand days and just couldn't see paying even such a sweet gal. The years since last they'd had a drink together had been kind to old Ruby. She'd filled out some, but the added curves didn't distract from her considerable charm. Ruby had matured into a statuesque brunette with a flawless ivory complexion. She still had all her pearly white teeth and her cameo features were unmarked by the life she'd led, which

18

was sort of astounding when you studied on it. Madame Moustache had worked hell out of of her gals when the trail herds were in town.

Ruby was tastefully dressed in a black velvet dress with a gray linen travel duster over it. The big black hat was a mite fancier than he liked, but he could see that it was tasteful and costly, too.

Ruby said, "I'm going to Salt Lake City, Custis. Where's this Tollwhatever you're getting off at?"

He sighed. "Just this side of the Divide—if we ever get there. I ain't drunk, Miss Ruby. I'm staring at you owly-eyed because I never got to sleep last night."

"You do look like someone dragged you through the keyhole backwards, honey. I'm rich these days, so I booked me a compartment up forward. Would you like to lie down a spell? I know *I* would."

Longarm stared at her as he digested her kind offer. Then he smiled crookedly and said, "Lord give me strength. I'm supposed to be on duty. I ain't herding cows no more, Miss Ruby. I'm working for Uncle Sam as a deputy U. S. marshal."

"So I've heard. I'm not in the same line of work as I was in Dodge, either, Longarm. That's what they call you now, isn't it?"

"That's right. So you've changed your business, too? I reckon we've all advanced in the world some since we was young and foolish in Dodge. What are you doing for a living these days, Miss Ruby? I can see by your outfit it must pay."

Ruby laughed. "I'm in the widow business. Do you remember old Silas Foster, the beef buyer in Dodge?"

"Sure. He was a nice old gent, as I recall."

"I liked him, too. He took me outten Madame Moustache's and made an honest woman outten me. I've been living in Chicago the last few years as a lady of high society. Ain't that a joke?"

Longarm chuckled. "It happens that way sometimes. I'm sure glad for you, Miss Ruby. But if you're a widow . . .?"

19

"Silas died the year before last. It's not true I caused his early demise, the way some of his sassy relatives suspicion. Silas done right by me and I done my duty as his wedded wife."

"I'm sure his last years must have been happy, Miss Ruby."

She grinned roguishly and confided, "I always have been warm-natured. But that's not what killed him. The doctor said he just got old. I must say I was starting to notice that towards the end. I was tempted more'n once to fool around on the side, but I never did. I made a bargain and I kept it." She shot him a thoughtful look and added, "But a girl has feelings, and my husband's been dead a spell, if you follow my drift."

"I do, and I feel honored as hell," Longarm said.

"Then what are we doing in this ridiculous vertical position, Longarm? Come on, let's go on up to my compartment and get to know one another better. I'll confess I always liked you, and you could have had me free in Dodge, if you hadn't been so shy."

She rose, so he had to, also. But he said warningly, "I don't think we'd better tempt fate, Miss Ruby. It's obvious the Lord just never meant for you and me to be more than pals."

"Have you gotten religion since last we met?"

"Not enough to act that foolish over, Miss Ruby. What I mean is that fate has diddled me again. Back in Dodge there were too many gents standing in line ahead of me, and now that we meet again I'm half asleep and fixing to get off the train so soon we'd only wind up disappointed as all hell."

She took his arm and said, "Somehow I doubt that, honey. Come on, let's finish this conversation in my compartment and out of these duds!"

He went with her. He figured he still had enough strength to overpower her in a wrestling match, if it had been polite to wrestle a she-male aboard a railroad train. But it wasn't, so he had to let her drag him the full length of the infernal train to her private compartment.

She shoved him down on the bunk and locked the door behind her as she tossed her hat aside and said, "I've been waiting a long time for this moment, Longarm."

"I sure wish you'd leave them buttons of yourn alone, Miss Ruby. Like I said, I'm supposed to be on *duty!*"

But Ruby LaRue was showing him that while she might have reformed some since her days at Madame Moustache's in Dodge, she still knew how to shed her duds faster than less worldly ladies would have considered possible.

It was broad day out and nothing was left to Longarm's imagination as Ruby folded her duster and dress neatly, put them aside, and proceeded to peel out of her black lace undergarments, bold as brass. When she got down to nothing but her high silk stockings she faced him, hands on hips, and asked, smiling saucily, "Well, here I am, and it's all yours. Are you still sleepy, handsome?"

Longarm laughed. "Not hardly," he said as he started to unbutton his trousers. Ruby dropped to her knees in front of him to help. As she opened him up down the front, Longarm tossed his Stetson aside and unbuckled his gun rig to tuck it between the mattress and the mahogany head of the bunk.

She opened the fly of his brown wool trousers and observed, "Hmm, I see you carry more than one weapon— and you're armed better than I had any right to dream!"

She grabbed his rigid, virile member, bent her head to kiss it, and murmured, "Oh, I've always wanted to meet you, you sweet thing!"

Longarm had to get out of the rest of his duds the best way he could manage, as Ruby proceeded to give him a French lesson that woke him up completely. By the time he'd struggled out of everything but his boots he was about to explode in her mouth, but he had a better place in mind. So he shoved her back and, as Ruby rolled on her ample, pale derriere and lay flat on the rug-covered floor, Longarm dove atop her.

Ruby spread her big white thighs and long, silk-sheathed

lower limbs to receive the bounty a kind fate had provided for a lonely widow woman.

She closed her eyes and moaned with pleasure as he entered her and kept going until their pubic bones were pressed together hard, tingling to the clickety-clack of the steel wheels rolling under them. She bit down with her experienced internal muscles and Longarm ejaculated hard inside her without having to really move enough to matter. Ruby laughed and said, "I felt that. I thought you said you were too tired, Custis."

"Honey, no man who's still able to breathe could be *that* tired! If I'd known, back in Dodge, how good you were, I'd have been proud to pay!"

Ruby laughed. "I'm glad we waited. Now we have time to do it right and just for the pure pleasure of it. Could you sort of move a mite, honey?"

"Sorry, I forgot my manners. Is that better?"

"Heavenly. The way the train wheels tingle my tailbone is doing something nice to me, too. Could you move up a little and . . . Oh, yes, that's perfect. Don't stop. Don't ever stop. I think I'm . . . *commmmming!*"

She wrapped her silk-sheathed ankles around him and hugged hard as hell as she wig-wagged her naked behind on the vibrating firm flooring. Longarm was glad they'd waited, too. Had he been paying for anything this nice, he'd have been sure she was faking her pleasure to make him feel flattered. As it was, it was hard to believe any gal could make her orgasm last like that. By the time she went limp and lay panting, flushed pink from her face down to her big, firm breasts, Longarm was reinspired and moving pretty good himself.

Ruby sighed and asked, "Could we get up on the bunk now, dear? A little of this prickly rug goes a long way."

He excused himself for being thoughtless, dismounted, and rose to haul her to her feet. They kissed standing face to face in the nude. That gave him an idea, but the coach was rocking too much to try. She laughed and moved away from him to climb onto the bunk. As he spied her carpet-rubbed pink derriere that gave him a better idea. Before she could roll over and lie down he stepped in, grabbed her hip bones, and entered her from behind, with her knees on the bunk and his booted feet on the floor.

She gasped. "Oh, nice! It goes in even deeper that way!"

That had been the general idea. It was also a more restful way for Longarm to move his hips pronto without having to deal with their weight. Now that the bloom was off the rose, he was starting to feel the altitude and lack of sleep. But he wasn't ready to quit. The scenery was too inspiring— both inside and out. The blinds were up, and if sure felt strange to be rutting like this in full view of the open range. He laughed as he spotted a white-faced cow staring in at them from a nearby ridge.

Looking down at Ruby's rear view was more interesting. She was face down on the linen and was moaning again as she arched her spine to present her high, curvaceous rump for full inspection and anything else he might want to do to it. He held her hip bones just below her trim, narrow waist, and leaned back to watch his erection plunging in and out of her. She begged him to move faster.

"Honey, I can't move any faster without losing my grasp of the situation," Longarm said. "I told you I was up all last night."

"Let me get on top, then," she suggested.

That sounded fair, so he let her. He knew as soon as his head rested on the pillow that he'd made a mistake. Ruby and his old organ grinder were still raring to go, but Longarm's weary head had been longing for a pillow and it was a pure bitch to keep his eyes open in this position. At least it was until old Ruby forked a leg over and settled on his shaft to go crazy some more.

"Do you like this?" she asked, as she started rocking faster. He laughed up at her bouncing breasts and then, not wanting her to hurt herself, took one in each hand to hold them safe while she moved her hips like a rider taking fences on a trotting horse.

This time they came together. Ruby fell limp in his arms

and lay still as their sex organs pulsed together in time to their hearts and the clicking wheels below.

Longarm sighed and fell asleep.

"...when we get to my hotel in Salt Lake—" Ruby breathed.

"Salt Lake? I got to get off at Tolland, Colorado!" gasped Longarm, waking up. He was making love to Ruby LaRue again.

He frowned and said, "Howdy. I must have dozed off."

Ruby said, "I noticed, but it don't matter. You're even good at this in your *sleep*, honey!"

He kept moving in her. Any man of mortal clay would have. But as his head began to clear, he noticed that the train wheels were slowing down. He reached up to yank the shades down as he said, "Jesus, we're coming to a town. I got to get up. I got to get dressed before this infernal train stops. Tolland's only a jerkwater stop. They won't stay there more'n a few minutes, and—"

"Don't stop," she pleaded. "I'm almost there again!"

He was, too. He knew they'd never forgive themselves if they stopped right now. But the train was going even slower. He said, "I hope we're coming into Pinecliffe. If it's Tolland I'm in trouble!"

"Faster, darling. Fast and hard! What difference does it make if you miss your fool stop? You can always catch the next train back, can't you?"

He started to say that was foolish, but as he felt himself swelling in pure pleasure inside her, he reconsidered. He could backtrack easily enough from Fraser or, hell, even Salt Lake City, when you studied on it. He knew that if he got off in Tolland after noon, as tired as he was, he wouldn't get enough done to matter before sundown. On the other hand, if he stole a day with this willing bawd, he'd be set to start out bright-eyed and bushy-tailed after a good night's sleep and other comforts. He laughed, kissed Ruby, and started moving faster. As the train rolled into Tolland and stopped with a hiss of steam and a whistle from the forward locomotive, Ruby sighed and said, "That was wonderful. I so wish you could ride all the way to Salt Lake with me, darling."

"I will," he said, "if you promise to let me sleep at least half the time."

She gripped him tighter with her body and laughed. "It's a deal. I was afraid you didn't like me enough to keep company with me that long. To tell you the truth, I'm sleepy, too, now."

Longarm pulled the covers up over them and, as Ruby nestled against him, they both closed their eyes as, unknown to them, two killers lay in wait for Longarm just outside.

Lynx and Spud stood at opposite ends of the platform, looking innocent but feeling worried. Nobody seemed to be getting off the train. Then, as the whistle sounded and the train was just starting up again, a tall man carrying a carpetbag swung down from one of the rear coaches. He didn't look very much like Longarm, but he was tall, wore a suit between his boots and Stetson, and had a moustache. Since he was facing Spud's way, Lynx shot him in the back.

Dogs barked and windows and doors started popping open as the two killers ran for their ponies. Nobody stopped them. The train was going one way and the killers were riding the other by the time someone finally rolled the murdered stranger over and asked, "Does anyone know him?" Aboard the train, the sleeping Longarm hadn't even heard the shots.

A mile outside of town, the killers reined in on a rise to look back and see if anyone was chasing them. Lynx laughed and said, "See how easy it was? Let's walk our mounts a spell to leave no dust agin the sky. By the time they forms a posse we'll be across the county line."

"I told you I'd been in this line of work a spell," Spud said. "I can see we done it right. But are you sure that was Longarm?"

"Who else could it have been? Wait till the boss hears. With Longarm dead, there's no chance he'll ever get caught.

25

The boss'll likely give us a nice bonus for this day's work, Spud."

By the time Longarm woke up to kiss Ruby some more, the two killers had made it almost to the mining town of Peacock. They were met by a man in black on a tall black stud.

He waved and the two killers joined him under an archway of dark, brooding spruce trees. Lynx reined in, saying, "We done it, boss. You don't have to worry about Longarm no more."

The boss nodded soberly. "I knew I could count on you boys. Are you sure he's really dead?"

"Hell, yes, we're sure. I half emptied my gun into his back at point-blank range. Ask Spud, here, if you don't believe me!"

Spud nodded. "I was watching his face when the bullets hit him from behind. If he wasn't dead before his face hit them planks, I've never seen a dead man's eyes before!"

"I never miss at ten feet," Lynx added modestly.

"You two ride on into town, then," the boss said. "I'll meet you later in the usual back room. Meanwhile, I'll ride back over your trail a mile or so, looking innocent, to find out if you've been followed."

Lynx grinned slyly. "I follows your drift, boss. Come on, Spud; I'll buy you a drink in town."

Spud agreed they were in a dry-mouthed line of work. So the two killers rode on as the boss made room for them. They didn't ride far. As soon as both their backs were turned to him, the boss pulled his primed carbine from its saddle boot and blew them both forward out of their saddles. As he steadied his spooked mount, gazing down at the bodies, while their own mounts galloped down the slope toward Peacock, the boss could see that they both looked dead. But he took careful aim and put a deliberate bullet in each of their skulls just to make sure.

Then, as he'd promised, he rode off looking innocent. With Lynx and Spud out of the way, there was nothing to connect him with the murder of Deputy U. S. Marshal Custis Long. And with Longarm dead, there was nothing to connect him to that unfortunate incident in Cheyenne a few years back.

He hadn't been caught that time. But Longarm had worked on the case and might or might not have suspected him. As Lynx and Spud had just discovered the hard way, the man who'd hired them was not one to take even moderate risks. Whether Longarm would have remembered him and questioned him about that old case or not was now a moot point.

He'd been keeping track of the time since gunning his confederates. So when the time was right he reined in, lit a smoke, and headed back up the trail toward the bodies, feeling sort of smug. Sure enough, when he got back within sight of the archway on the rise, he saw men from town crowded under the spruces. As the murderer joined the others who'd responded to the sounds of gunplay just outside of town, he called out, "What's going on, boys? I heard a mess of shots up this way. Sounded like rifle fire."

As the killer joined the mostly mounted crowd around the bodies, a dismounted man wearing a gray walrus moustache and a mail-order town marshal's badge spat and answered, "You heard right. Take a gander at these gents on the ground and speak up if you've any notion who they might be. They ain't from Peacock."

One of the other men in the crowd spoke up to say, "I've seen that checker vest afore, Marshal. The dead man wearing it was drinking in the Silver Spade the other night."

The killer nodded. "I've seen them both before, too. Matter of fact, they both asked me for jobs in that same drinking establishment. I disremember either of 'em offering me a sensible name. One of 'em called himself Link or something. Naturally, I didn't hire 'em. They looked sort of worthless."

The town marshal said, "They do read sort of saddle tramp. But it's still agin the law to gun folks on this trail.

27

We'd best carry these boys into Peacock and put 'em on ice till the county coroner can have a look-see."

There was a chorus of agreement. But before anyone could do anything, they all heard the sound of approaching hoofbeats. A mess of hoofbeats. There was over a dozen riders in the posse from Tolland.

As the newcomers reined in, the deputy sheriff from Tolland spied Spud's checkered vest and yelled, "Hot damn! That's one of 'em! The Widow Phalan says one was wearing a checky vest!"

The marshal of Peacock looked up with a slight frown. "Howdy, boys. Ain't you sort of over the county line?"

The leader of the Tolland lawmen said, "Screw the county line. We was in hot pursuit. And you know what them rascals done? They just gunned a deputy U. S. marshal as he was getting off the train back in Tolland!"

The killer repressed a smile as he pointed at a glitter in the grass just off the trail. "Hey, that looks like spent brass, yonder."

So the town marshal of Peacock dashed over to pick up the ejected shell from the killer's Winchester as the killer casually asked the deputy from Tolland, "Are you sure these were the killers? Who was the gent they murdered, again?"

The Tolland deputy was watching the local law as he replied. "Sure, we're sure. The whole damn town saw them running for their ponies after they gunned the pore fed. His name was Long. The one from Denver they call Longarm. We knowed it was him 'cause we was expecting him to get off that train, and he did. We've already wired the U. S. marshal in Denver. They asked us to ship his body home on the next eastbound, so we will."

The killer whistled softly. "Good Lord, these rascals gunned the famous Longarm? I met him one time, up Cheyenne way. He was a good old boy, and they said he never forgot a face."

The Peacock marshal held the spent brass up to the light and snapped, "Shit, it's a Winchester .44-40 round!"

"I was afraid of that," the killer said. "That's the most

28

common ammo in these parts. Matter of fact, I'm packing a .44-40 myself."

There was a chorus of agreement from the others gathered around. The marshal tossed the brass away. "Well, this sure is getting to be a pure mystery," he said. "These gents on the ground add up as the killers of that U. S. deputy. But I doubt like hell they committed suicide out of remorse."

"Hell, I suspect I can put her together for you," the killer said. "Like I said, Longarm never forgot a face, and we all agree that these jaspers were a pair of no-good drifters. They must have been on the dodge. They asked for work up here near the timberline, got turned down, and were fixing to move on when they run into Longarm in Tolland. He had them on his list, but this time he lost, when all concerned slapped leather on sight!"

"That makes sense. But then who gunned Longarm's killers? It sure wasn't Longarm!"

The killer said, "That's easy. There was a third man riding with them. We know he has to have been an ornery killer. So he likely stayed out of sight whilst his sidekicks scouted the Tolland depot. After the killing the three rode off together. But the smarter one knew there was no place three strangers could go up here without being noticed. On the other hand, one stranger don't stand out as much. And, remember, he knew nobody in Tolland had seen *him* when Longarm was killed. So..."

"Hot damn, that makes sense. The third rider kilt these two and rode off, trying to look innocent without the burden of his trigger-happy sidekicks!"

The killer smiled. "There you go, boys. Now all we have to do is to find a stranger in these parts who can't account for himself at the time of either shootout."

The deputy from Tolland laughed. "By gum, that works. We know the time on all three killings. Let's circle out and see if we can cut the rascal's sign. We know he didn't ride neither way along this hoof-pounded trail, for had he, you boys from Peacock or us boys from Tolland would have met him on it."

The killer nodded and said, "That's right. But while we're jawing about him here, the son of a bitch is getting farther away by the minute. So let's start looking for him pronto. Old Longarm was a pal of mine."

Chapter 3

When a rider finds himself caught in an unexpected stampede, he tends to forget that the original chore was to drive the herd in some particular direction. But by the time they arrived in Salt Lake City that night, Longarm had caught up on his sleep and other creature comforts and was feeling a mite guilty about sleeping—among other things—on the job.

He felt even dumber when he spied the headlines of the *Deseret News*. There was a paper and tobacco counter in the lobby of Ruby's hotel. So, while she verified her reservation at the desk, Longarm moseyed over innocently to buy a paper and some extra smokes with his back to the room clerk. He felt dumb being signed in as a dead beef buyer from Chicago. Besides, he'd once checked in here under a different name with a different gal.

Western Union moved news dispatches across the Great Divide a lot faster than the D&RG Western could move trains. So the *Deseret News* had the sad tale of Longarm's death by gunfire in Tolland. Longarm bought a copy and read it with chagrin. He'd had to explain a lot to Billy Vail in the past, but explaining *this* was going to be one pure bitch!

Ruby joined him. "We're all set, honey. We got us a room with a bath, and I'm looking forward to doing it with you in a tub."

"I'll take you up and let you get started with your buttons," he said. "But before I touch any of mine, I got me a mess of telegrams to send. You did say I'm checked in as the late Silas Foster?"

"Of course. I had the reservation as Mrs. Silas Foster, so who else could a respectable gal like me take private baths with? Who do you have to wire, honey?"

He showed her the paper. "My poor old Uncle Billy. He'll be home at this hour. I don't want him losing sleep over this fool mix-up."

Ruby whistled softly and said, "My God, you're supposed to have walked into an ambush back at Tolland!"

"I already read that. What I have to figure out now is who the hell got shot in my place. The paper says my body's been sent back to Denver. The gent they shot must not have had any identification. That's odd, too, when you study on it."

Ruby took his arm. "Let's talk about it upstairs in bed. I'm no law-gal, but I think I can see what happened. You owe me your hide, you sweet thing. Had not I led you down the primrose path..."

"I said I had some of it figured," Longarm said. "You go on up and leave me a light in the window whilst I run over to the Western Union."

She repeated the room number, kissed his cheek, and went upstairs.

The Western Union office was only a block down Main Street. Longarm sent a straight wire that Billy Vail would get within the hour.

EARLIER REPORTS EXAGGERATED STOP AM AT BEEHIVE HOTEL SALT LAKE AS SILAS FOSTER STOP WHAT WAS IN BOX THEY SENT YOU QUESTION MARK

Then, having done his duty for the moment, Longarm went back to the hotel and took a hot tub bath with Ruby. The warm water eased his saddle sores some, but he could hardly say that a long hot soak with Ruby was a restful experience. They got a lot of water on the bathroom tiles before he had her calmed down again for a while. She dried off and leaped into the big brass bed with a sassy suggestion, but Longarm put on his pants and shirt, explaining that he was expecting company.

He had timed it neatly. He had just made himself decent and lit a smoke when a knock came on the door. He let the Western Union messenger boy in and told him to have a seat and be still while he pondered his next move. Marshal Vail's wired reply read:

WHAT ARE YOU DOING IN SALT LAKE QUES-
TION MARK PRESENT YOU SENT WAS TOTAL
STRANGER STOP HAVE YOU LOST YOUR
MIND ENTIRE QUESTION MARK

Longarm chuckled, asked the messenger for his pad and pencil, and wrote back:

DIVERSIONARY TACTICS STOP INTEND TO
SHOW UP INCOGNITO FOR OBVIOUS REA-
SONS STOP CHECKING LEAD IN SALT LAKE
STOP WILL HEAD BACK DIRECTLY STOP YOUR
LOVING NEPHEW

He paid off the messenger and sent him on his way. As he shut the door after him, Ruby came up from under the covers and asked if they were likely to be interrupted again in the near future. He said not for at least an hour or so. So she threw off the covers, rolled over on her hands and knees, and presented her ample derriere, explaining, "I can't seem to get enough of it from you, honey. I don't know if it's the nice way you do it or if I'm coming down with

33

something, but it sure feels good."

He sat on the bed and commenced to peel. "We'd best start pacing ourselves, Ruby," he said. "It's the altitude that's making you so horny. You been living in Chicago, closer to sea level. You ain't used to the thin air out here."

"Is that why I get so excited? I thought it was passion. Whatever it is, I want some more."

He finished undressing, but rolled her on her side to hold her in his arms gently as he said, "We got longer than I figured, so let's make it last."

"Oh, you do mean to spend the whole night with me, dear? I thought you said you had to hop the midnight train back."

He took the cheroot from between his lips, kissed her, and let her puff on it as he explained. "I've been studying on that notion. If some rascals were waiting for me to get off the westbound passenger combination, they expected me to arrive that way. By now they might or might not know they gunned the wrong victim. I ain't sure I want to give 'em another shot at me by climbing down from the eastbound passenger combination at a lonely hour."

"Oh, good. You can stay here with me then. My business here in Salt Lake will keep us in this nice hotel for the better part of a week, and—"

"Hold on," he cut in with a laugh. "You wouldn't get much of your cattle buying done and I wouldn't get a damned *thing* done if we followed that suggestion. No offense, Ruby, but we can't stay together like this forever, or even another twenty-four hours."

"But you will give me at least this night in heaven, honey?"

"Yep. Angels deserve no less, and if you didn't turn out to be my guardian angel today, I never met one before." He chuckled. "It just goes to show that virtue ain't always its own reward after all."

He snubbed out the cheroot and started to haul the covers up over them, for Salt Lake nights had a nip to them, even in summer.

Ruby asked, "Can't we do it one more time before we go to sleep?"

He started to protest. There were limits to any man's endurance, and while Ruby was a handsome as well as skilled lover, she was just too insatiable for him. But she was fooling with his privates while begging for more loving, and he began to find himself rising to the occasion. Still, in truth, it was starting to become more work than pleasure by the time he'd made her come again.

He asked if it was all right with her if he caught forty winks now. Ruby started crying. He held her closer and asked, "What's wrong? Didn't I pleasure you that time?"

She sobbed. "You know you did. But I can tell that you're starting to lose interest. You men are all alike, once a gal's given you her all. Now that you're satisfied you're having second thoughts about my past, ain't you?"

He patted her bare shoulder soothingly. "Honey, I'm more worried about my future than I am about your past. You've wrung me out like a dishrag, and some rascals with guns seem to be laying for me in Tolland. I got too much on my mind to study on the old days in Dodge."

She sniffed. "But you do remember me from Dodge as a working gal, don't you?"

"I'd forgotten, till you brought it up."

"I'll just bet you had. No man ever forgets when a gal has been a low-down whore!"

"Oh, hell, Ruby, you were never a low-down whore. Madame Moustache charged top dollar. Besides, you ain't been a whore for quite a spell."

"I bet you still think I'm wicked, though."

"Hell, girl, you *are* wicked. So am I. That's nothing to be ashamed of. Wicked gals are the only ones I like to mess with, and if you'd been a prissy schoolmarm I'd likely be dead right now instead of just screwed weak."

Ruby chuckled but murmured wistfully, "It's different with men. Men are expected to be horny old brutes. Everyone looks down on gals who let their feelings show."

He held her closer, fondling one of her breasts as he

answered. "Don't talk dumb. Any fair-minded person can see that us horny men couldn't exercise our franchise to sow wild oats if at least some of you pretty little things didn't cooperate. It seems to me no man has a right to call any she-male wickeder than himself unless he saves all his loving for his own fool fist, and they say *that's* a crime against nature, too."

She reached down between them. "I'd best do it for you, then. I wouldn't want you feeling ashamed."

He laughed. "Honey, what you're fondling ain't capable at this moment of feeling anything. Let's go to sleep."

So they did, for a while. But it was still dark out when Longarm woke up with Ruby on top of him, acting wicked again. There was nothing he could do about it, since she'd revived his hard feelings from the dead with her skilled gyrations. But after he put her back to sleep again, purring like a contented pussy, Longarm gingerly slipped out of bed and got dressed so he could get some rest.

He tiptoed out, knowing Ruby would be upset when she awoke to find him gone. But every such meeting of passing ships tended to end sort of wistfully, and Longarm found tearsome goodbyes a tedious chore.

Out on the streets the dawn was cold and gray. The morning breeze off the big salty lake to the west tasted refreshing and he knew he was really awake for keeps now.

Despite all the loving, Longarm had gotten more sleep in the past few hours than he was generally used to. But the intervals of loving had left him hungry as a wolf. So he found an all-night beanery down by the railyards and ordered ham, eggs, and chili with a mug of coffee. The waitress said she could see by his drinking coffee that he was no Mormon. When he apologized for his lack of faith, she said she was no Mormon, either, and she said it sort of sultry.

They were alone in the beanery. The waitress was pretty and filled her thin cotton uniform nicely indeed. She allowed she'd be getting off in less than an hour and, without Longarm's asking, volunteered that she lived nearby, alone.

She looked sort of sore when he laughed.

"I ain't laughing at you," he said. "I'm laughing at me. I can't hang about to walk you home, and some night in a lonesome sleeping bag on the range I'm going to cuss like hell about that."

"I know the feeling. But, listen, if you'll be in town a day or so, and want my address..."

He wrote it down to be polite. Then he left her a whole two bits as a tip to make her feel that he really admired her. He was still laughing about it as he walked over to the railyards and hunted down a train dispatcher he knew.

The dispatcher said he could put Longarm and a hired mount aboard a cattle train heading east in about an hour and said he could ask the crew to stop in open country, as Longarm asked, if there was a good reason.

There was. Longarm wanted to get off mounted and well clear of any regular stop where bushwhackers might be lying for him. The dispatcher shook on it. So now all Longarm needed was a horse. He'd checked his saddle, possibles, and Winchester in the baggage car coming west, so they were waiting for him at the depot just down the tracks.

As he strode over to the nearest police station on North Temple he had time to ponder some. The rascals who'd gunned another man in his place could not have known his face on sight, but the mysterious cadaver had matched his description closely enough. Longarm knew he had a reputation, so lots of folk knew he favored a McClellan Army saddle. When he found a Salt Lake copper badge he could trust and laid out his problem, the Salt Lake police department was willing to lend him a chestnut police horse and a battered but serviceable double-rigged stock saddle.

By the time he arranged to have his original saddle sent back to Denver and got his borrowed mount aboard an empty cattle car near the caboose of the eastbound combination, the train was fixing to leave. Longarm rode in the caboose with the brakemen. It would have been tedious as hell, since the long climb back was slower than a cat shitting through a funnel, but a crew chief said Longarm could sleep atop the covers of his own bunk, since he was paid to sort of watch things as they rolled.

So Longarm caught up even more on his sleep and woke up bright-eyed and bushy-tailed well before they reached the Divide again. He had coffee and beans with the friendly railroad men while he asked their views on the robberies along the narrow-gauge north of the main line. They had lots of opinions, but none Longarm could use. He already knew that for some fool reason the Timberliners were passing up the plunder on the main east-west line. But the notion that the robbers were using a handcar or even a ghost locomotive sounded mighty wild. Longarm had noticed in the past that folks who robbed for a living seldom played chess when the name of the game was checkers. There had to be some simple reason why they concentrated on the private narrow-gauge. When he figured that part out, he'd likely know who was doing it.

Late that afternoon the train stopped up above timberline, in a stretch it wasn't supposed to, and Longarm swore the crew to silence as he got his borrowed chestnut off and mounted up. He rode well clear of the tracks and braced himself in the unfamiliar saddle as he waited to see what the unfamiliar mount would do when the train started up again.

The chestnut didn't do anything. He just twitched his ears as the train left, clanking and hissing no worse than the street cars and such the chestnut was used to down in Salt Lake. Longarm patted his neck and said, "We're going to get along, Copper. Let's see if we can find that narrow-gauge railhead at Peacock before the sun goes down."

They left the tracks, trending north-northeast along the natural grain of the high lonesome. The range above timberline was carpeted with alpine grass and bitty flowers growing between outcrops of gray granite. It looked sort of like a big rock garden sloping gently to the east. The skyline rode close and sharp-edged to his left, for he was perhaps a mile east of the Divide itself. Off to his right, the world just went on forever till it sort of fuzzed itself out somewhere on the high plains. Between them and the tawny dull gold of the distant prairie, row after row of north-south ridges formed a vast giant's stairway with the parks and vales between hidden by the shade of the low afternoon sun to the west. The first ridge to his right was as bare as the one he was following, though some juniper and wind-tortured spruce grew scattered along the bottom of the draw between. Past the bare high country keeping company with him, the lower ridges were dull blue with trees too tiny to count from up here. Up ahead a high peak stood snow-covered against the northern sky.

That figured to be Arapahoe Mountain. He twisted in the saddle and looked back. Yep, that had to be Jame's Peak behind him. He wasn't aiming to climb either, but it was comforting to know where he was. Feeling the lay of the land was sort of like swimming. Once you'd ridden over a stretch one time it started coming back to you as you just moved naturally. He'd ridden this range a couple of times before, so he knew he couldn't get lost.

But Peacock could. He'd been up here looking for owl-hoots, not towns. Thus, while he had himself right on the map, he wasn't exactly sure where Peacock might be. He knew this trail would eventually take him to Cameron Pass north of Sawtooth. But that was way north of where Billy Vail had told him to go. So he started looking for a side trail down to the low vale to his right. He knew the little town of Peacock had to be there somewhere. He was well north of Tolland. Billy Vail had mentioned a stage from Tolland to Peacock, but all he could see down there in this tricky light was a mess of misty darkness. He knew if he rode down to the wagon trace it had to lead him on to Peacock, but he didn't want to approach Peacock from the south. That was the way they would be expecting him to come, if they had figured out by now that they'd ambushed the wrong man.

The morning papers hadn't said so. Marshal Vail was playing slick about the mysterious stranger in the Denver morgue. But Longarm knew that mysterious strangers tended to have friends and relations. The gent they'd killed had gotten off the train. So he'd had some business in the high country. By now, all sorts of folks could be asking why he never showed up. Once word got around that a gent answering more or less to Longarm's description was missing, the killers would have to be mighty dumb not to reconsider who they might have gunned back in Tolland.

Longarm rode the chestnut between two big frost-battered boulders. As he got a better view to the north, he nodded and told his mount, "That has to be Peacock a couple of miles north, unless it's a brush fire."

The shadowy vale ahead lay under a shroud of thick, evil yellow-brown foundry smoke. The smoke was all one could see from higher up, but there wasn't any other place near enough to mention where they refined ore. Longarm let his mount graze as he lit some smoke of his own and studied the view. Then he heeled the chestnut forward, saying, "Come on, we'll pass high, hit the narrow-gauge north of town, and backtrack in from the north, like we've been picnicking or something."

It took longer than anyone but an experienced mountain rider like Longarm would have expected. Distances were tricky up here, and they still had some serious alpine range to cover before the smoke-filled vale lay south-southeast of them and the silvery tracks of the narrow-gauge lay directly downslope. Longarm swung his mount down the gentle incline as he studied the tracks. He noticed it was a single line. The little trains ran only one way at a time. So there went all those bright notions about handcars. Glancing to his right, he saw that the tracks branched out into a railyard just this side of the smoke-shrouded mining town. The other way, the single line just followed a wavy contour line up a nine-degree grade to vanish into a tunnel cut through a granite buttress nature had provided the Great Divide without consulting any railroad engineers.

Longarm wondered if he should check out that tunnel before riding on into Peacock. The reports on the holdups hadn't said that any had taken place close to town, and from

Peacock on a clear day, one could see the mouth of said tunnel, so what the hell.

Then, even as he stared at it, a dinky Shay locomotive burst out of the tunnel mouth like a bull on fire. It was coming down the grade lickety-split, like it aimed to get to town in a hurry. Longarm gauged the speed of the train, the grade of the tracks, and the fact that while the diamond stack was smoking, it wasn't puffing sensibly. So he swore, kicked hard, and yelled, "*Move,* Copper! We got us a train to catch!"

The train was going a hell of a lot faster than any horse could run on the level, of course, but Longarm and his chestnut had a lead and a downhill run. So they made it—just. The well trained police mount fell into step with the pounding counterweights of the little engine's drivers as the runaway locomotive overtook them. They'd never have beaten the cow catcher far, but Longarm managed to catch the grab irons of the cab and haul himself out of the saddle and into the engineer's usual surroundings.

The engineer and fireman didn't seem to be there. Longarm hadn't expected to find anyone sensible at the controls. He grabbed the brake handle in one hand and threw the reverse lever with the other. Then he opened the throttle wide to feed steam.

Now the cars behind him were sliding on locked wheels and the Shay's drivers were screaming like tin banshees as they churned the track in reverse. It was still a near thing. The train took forever to slow down enough to matter. They were still going way too fast when they whizzed into the yards of Peacock. Longarm saw startled faces outside. He felt sort of startled himself when he looked out ahead and saw that they were running out of track. They were pig-squealing along a dead-end siding. But while the tracks ended less than a quarter of a mile ahead, a little red school-house lay bull's-eye just beyond the fence at the end of the yards.

Sure hope school's out! Longarm said to himself as he braced himself, feeding steam. He knew that anyone with

41

a lick of sense would be jumping from the cab about now. But the steam throttle had a dead-man's switch, and the moment he let go the drivers would stop reversing. And he sure needed some reversing right now.

So he stayed with the ship, and for a time it looked like he was going to go up with it. Exploding locomotives could hardly be said to go down. But there were limits, after all, to how far a train could slide against inertia, and by the time the cow catcher hit and demolished the heavy timber balks at the end of the line and allowed the little sharp-edged wheels of the pilot to sink to their axles into the softer earth beyond, inertia gave up.

The train came to rest in a billowing cloud of dust, smoke, and steam, with its cow catcher poking through the fence and its headlamp staring owlishly at the little red schoolhouse.

A side door opened and a pretty young gal in a calico dress popped out to stare at the locomotive facing her at spitting distance. She screamed and ran back inside. Some women were like that. Anyone could see he'd stopped the infernal train before it could join her in the schoolroom after hours.

Longarm swung out to stare up the track for his mount. He spied old Copper following sedately, at a modest walk for a horse who ran so good. Longarm saw that there were four cars behind the tender, too. But he seemed to be all alone on the train.

The same could not be said for the railyards all around. More men than he could shake a stick at were running across the tracks toward him from every direction. Some of them were waving guns.

Chapter 4

Longarm swore, disgusted. For a man who'd aimed to enter Peacock unobserved, he'd sure done one hell of a job.

He swung down from the cab as a gray-edged gent with a mail-order badge on his vest ran up with an old Colt Dragoon trained on the world in general.

Longarm kept his hands polite as he said, "Now, don't get your bowels in an uproar, Constable. I don't know why this train was in such a hurry, neither. I spied her coming down the mountain with no hand on her throttle and swung aboard. Now you know as much as me."

"No, I don't," the older lawman said. "I'm Town Marshal Bordon, not a constable—and who in thunder are you?"

Longarm hesitated. He hadn't planned on arriving so spectacularly. On the other hand, the old gent looked proddy enough to insist on some I.D., and that Dragoon in his liver-spotted hand was making Longarm nervous.

"I'm law, too," Longarm said. "I'm a deputy U. S. marshal sent to look into the train robbing up this way. From the looks of things, I'd say one must have just taken place."

It worked, for now. The town law yelled, "Dave, Steve—check the mail car! Pete—run back and see if anyone's aboard the coaches!"

Some gents who figured to be his deputies ran up the

tracks to do as the town law said, while even more Peacockers joined Longarm and Bordon. A tall gent wearing a business suit and a vaguely familiar face came closer, blinked in utter astonishment, and gasped, "Longarm! We thought you were dead!"

Longarm wanted to kick him. Instead he shrugged and said, "Well, there goes the ball game. Do I know you, friend?"

"I'm Tom Carrol," the tall stranger said. "Don't you remember me? We worked on the same case a few years back."

Marshal Bordon shook his head as if he'd been punched and said, "I had you down as dead, too. This is confusing as hell. But if Tom says he knows you, that's good enough for me."

Longarm didn't answer. He'd put the name and the face together now. He held out his hand. "Howdy, Tom Carrol. I got you placed now. You was working as a railroad dick for the U.P., right?"

"That's me. Did you ever catch up with those boys who were robbing the mail on the U.P. Flyer?"

"No, but they stopped. What are you doing up here these days, Tom? Working for the narrow-gauge as a security man?"

"That's about the size of it, Longarm. What say we all go over to the saloon to catch up on the past few years more comfortably? It's mighty dusty around here now, thanks to you."

Longarm had better things to do than belly up with a railroad dick he barely remembered. "I got to get my mount rubbed down and put away safe for the night," he said. "Got to find some quarters for myself, too."

Marshal Bordon said, "You're staying at my house. You go along with old Tom and I'll join you once I get a handle on things here. My boys will see to your mount. But wait in the saloon for me, hear? I got some questions to ask, too, once I figure out what the hell is going on."

Longarm let Tom Carrol lead him across the yards to the

nearest drinking establishment. They were followed by more curious townspeople than Longarm would have invited to come along, if he'd had anything to say about the matter.

It was an ugly little town under its overcast of perpetual foundry smoke. Longarm asked the railroad dick where they got the coal and Carrol said there was a coal mine up the tracks as well as some lead, zinc, silver, and even a little gold. As they entered the saloon and bellied up to the bar, Carrol explained, "The silver is all anyone's making money on right now. Lead and zinc are both down, and we're too far from the market to make it worth while. What are we drinking, Longarm?"

"Beer, if you're buying. I've a feeling we may have us a long night."

Carrol ordered as Longarm studied his profile. It was coming back to him now. He'd never paid much mind to the younger railroad dick on that old case, because he hadn't much reason to. Carrol hadn't been a suspect, but he hadn't been much help either. Longarm knew it was impolite to ask a private investigator where he'd gotten his training. Carrol's training hadn't been much, from the way he'd overlooked so many standard security moves for the U.P. That was likely why he was working for a mountain railroad these days instead of the U.P. It might explain why Uncle Sam had had to send a pro, too.

Things were looking up. Longarm picked up his schooner, clinked glass with Carrol, and swallowed some beer with a smile. If old Tom Carrol had checked out the recent robberies with the same skill as he had shown on that other case, there might not be such a mystery after all. Carrol looked and talked bright enough, but he seemed to be a piss-poor investigator. It was all coming back now. Longarm remembered the night Carrol and the other dicks working under him had messed up on that stakeout. But, as old Tom said, it had been a long time ago and it seemed impolite to tell the man who was buying that you thought he was a fool.

Carrol asked, "Did you hear about someone getting

45

gunned in your place in Tolland yesterday?"

Longarm shrugged. "Read something about it in the papers. As you can see, it wasn't me. Did you get a good look at the gent?"

"Hell, no. I'd have known he wasn't you if I had."

"That's good detecting, Tom. I'd ask if anyone in these parts might have recognized him, but that would be a dumb question. So he'll just have to stay on ice in Denver till we figure out who in hell he might have been."

A man on the other side of Longarm opined, "Someone in Denver ought to know who them other rascals was. Nobody in these parts ever seen 'em afore."

Longarm frowned. "Other rascals?"

The railroad dick took the ball back. "I thought you knew about them, Longarm. Right after you—I mean that other gent—was ambushed over in Tolland, two others was gunned just outside of Peacock."

The conversational townsman on Longarm's far side said, "They surely was. I was one of the first Peacockers on the scene. We found the rascals dead on the trail. Both shot in the back with a .44-40. Then the posse from Tolland rode up and said they was the men who'd shot Longarm. Excuse me—that other feller."

"He's right," Tom Carrol said. "I was there, too. As near as we could put it together, there must have been three in the gang. After they gunned that stranger in Tolland, they fell out over the matter and one of them gunned the other two. The one who got away was likely upset with his sidekicks for gunning such an important personage. So he blowed them outten their saddles, and by now he's either halfway to Mexico or halfway to Canada."

The railroad dick nodded and went on, "Nobody can say for sure if they was after you personal. But whatever that killing in Tolland was about, two of the rascals are dead and the other's run off scared skinny!"

Longarm sipped his beer and didn't answer. It wasn't smart to tell the world how smart you were. It seemed obvious to Longarm that some slick hired gun had used two dupes and then gunned them to cover his own trail. By now—or at the least before this night was over—the killer would know he'd ordered the wrong man murdered and would doubtless feel chagrined. Longarm had enough on his plate when—not if—the rascal tried again. So this was no time to announce that he was on the prod and braced for yet another attempt on his life. He owed the fact that he was still alive to his own weak nature and the killer making a natural mistake. Longarm could only hope he'd go on making mistakes.

He said, "Well, boys, let's forget about them doubtless confused saddle tramps and study on the gang I came up here to hunt. Have you been keeping records on what's been stolen off the robbed trains, Carrol?"

"Records?" asked the railroad dick, blank-faced.

Longarm sighed. "Records. Words on paper. Generally, after someone's been robbed, it's supposed to be recorded how much was taken from whom, when, where, and so forth."

"Oh, we know the dates and such," Carrol said. "As to exact figures, it ain't that easy. The Timberliners haven't taken anything from the few passengers or crewmen on the narrow gauge. They just seem interested in the mail car and what's in it."

"Tearing open the mail sacks was their federal mistake. But what else might there have been of value in those mail cars?" Longarm asked.

Carrol shrugged. "Raw gold and silver, mostly. That's why it's hard to tally exact figures. A poke of color or a sack of horn silver don't have a price tag till it's assayed and refined more here in Peacock."

Longarm frowned and said, "Hold on. Are you saying the Timberliners have been stealing *ore*? That's one hell of a lot of heavy work for such modest profit!"

Carrol shook his head. "It adds up. They ain't been messing with the gondolas of low-grade from the mines, Longarm. You see, as they works the veins, the miners come across poker chips of horn silver or nuggets of native gold. Naturally, stuff like that goes into sealed pokes to be shipped under guard."

Longarm took another sip of beer as he digested that. Native gold was easy to sell anywhere. Horn silver was bulkier and still needed modest refining before it was pure enough to coin or make silverware out of. But a pound of horn silver added up to perhaps three-quarters of a pound of sterling. He'd heard silver was down on the market. He'd have to check. Meanwhile, any silver at all was worth something, when you considered the low overhead the Timberliners had. He made a mental note to have Billy Vail check out fences who were known to keep a small but hot furnace on the premises. Horn silver was too bulky to carry far.

Before Longarm could ask about local foundries, another townie came in to yell, "They're comin' down the track! The folks who was on the train just made it back to town!"

Longarm finished his beer and followed the others back outside.

It was either getting late or the smoke above Peacock was getting thicker. It was hard to tell, in Peacock, whether the sun was still up or not. They had street lamps going night and day along the main streets and the overcast reflected a murky orange glow down on everything and everybody. Everyone in town seemed to be headed for the nearby railyards, so Longarm went, too. He elbowed his way through the crowd to join Marshal Bordon and the foot-sore refugees from the train he'd stopped just in time. He stood by Bordon and just listened as the engineer told everyone about the holdup.

He didn't say anything surprising. The train had been stopped six or seven miles north by a big boulder on the tracks. Thinking it had rolled down the slope to the west on its own, the engine crew had climbed down to lever it off. That was when a dozen-odd masked men had materialized from behind some other rocks and taken over as if they had studied under the James boys. Nobody had been hurt. The crew and half-dozen passengers had put up no fight. The Timberliners hadn't asked for their valuables.

They'd just been told to drop their gunbelts and start walking north along the tracks until further notice. Naturally, since the tracks were running uphill and the next town north was a tedious distance, the victims had stopped once they were out of sight of the train, had a smoke, and started back toward Peacock, moving slowly, until they'd found their guns where they'd left them and noticed that neither the robbers nor the purloined train were anywhere in sight.

Marshal Bordon said, "I can pick it up from there, boys. After looting the train they just let loose the brakes and let her roll. Had not this federal man, here, stopped her just in time, that fool Shay would have hit the schoolhouse going lickety-split!"

Everyone turned to Longarm and one of the townies slapped him on the back.

"Never mind about the parts we can answer," Longarm said. "I got some harder questions. You boys did say the train was coming down to Peacock when it stopped for a rock on the tracks, didn't you?"

"We did, and I'm madder than a hog in a cactus patch about it, too," the engineer said. "Them sons of bitches showed no consideration to my engine, sending her downhill like that."

"They did show unusual enterprise for men who don't cotton to honest work, though," Longarm said. "To let the Shay roll, they had to have moved that big rock out of the way. Aside from being hard work, it cost them time they could have used just putting some distance between themselves and the scene of their latest crime. I got to study on that rock. I've never known anyone who enjoyed shifting rock about. So they must have had a reason."

Tom Carrol said, "Hell, their reason's over yonder by the schoolhouse. The sons of bitches did it to be ornery!"

"Maybe," Longarm said. "Where did your boys put my mount, Marshal Bordon?"

Bordon called out, "Dave, go fetch Longarm's hoss!" He told Longarm, "It's getting too dark to cut sign. I'd wait till morning iffen I was you, Longarm."

"It's a good thing you ain't me, then," Longarm said. "A man can ride a long ways overnight. Did any of you boys on the train notice what kind of mounts the rascals had?"

The victims buzzed a bit before one man volunteered, "I can't say we saw any horses, Deputy. But they must have had some. They was long gone by the time we got back to where they stopped us."

Bordon added, "They *had* to ride out. A dozen men afoot would stand out like sore thumbs out on the high range."

Longarm didn't answer. A dozen men *riding* would have been noticed, had anyone been about to notice. Since they'd left the abandoned train with no witnesses watching, they could have ridden off on elephants for all it mattered.

The town deputy called Dave led Longarm's chestnut police mount across the yards. Longarm thanked him and mounted up.

Marshal Bordon asked, "Are you really riding out after them with nightfall coming down?"

Longarm said, "Why no, I thought I'd just ride up the tracks a ways to hear the hoot owls sing."

"Wait up. Me and the boys had best ride with you," the marshal said.

Longarm told them to catch up when and if, as he meant to ride slowly with his eyes peeled. He belied his words some by heeling Copper into a trot to get clear of the crowd and the other annoying distractions of Peacock.

He slowed Copper to a walk along the narrow-gauge once he was out from under the umbrella of foundry smoke. The light was better, but not much, for the sun had dropped behind the Divide to the west and the thin air up here didn't hold much afterglow. The sky was purple velvet and the scenery around him was mostly slate-gray with inky shadows. Peacock's valley lay just about at timberline, so unhappy-looking junipers stood here and there in the dim light.

He didn't look for sign at first, since he knew no robbers had been about when he'd seen that locomotive come bursting out of the tunnel up the grade. He was approaching the tunnel when he heard yells behind him and reined in to wait for the marshal and a handful of riders. As they fell in with him, Longarm noticed that the railroad dick, Tom Carrol, had tagged along.

He asked, "Carrol, are there any more trains due down the mountain tonight?"

Carrol said no and asked why. Longarm explained that riding through railroad tunnels on horseback could shorten a man's life if a train came along at the wrong time. Carrol assured him the tunnel was safe, so Longarm took the lead and they rode through.

The tunnel was longer and darker than Longarm had expected. He lit a match. There wasn't much to see. The rock walls rose on either side to form a vaulted ceiling that looked solid enough. But he saw spots where rock had fallen to leave divots of granite gray in the coating of smokestack soot up there. A cabbage-sized cobble landing on the top of a coach or an engine likely wouldn't hurt it much, but it was sobering to consider one landing on the crown on one's Stetson. So he heeled Copper forward to get out of there.

Beyond the tunnel, the tracks kept rising and the slopes got barer. The ground rose to their left and dropped off steeper to their right. By the time they reached the stretch where one of the riders who'd been on the train said they'd been stopped, the valley floor to the right lay hidden in inky shadows, a good five hundred feet lower than the tracks.

Longarm reined in and dismounted. He dropped to one knee and squinted up the tracks. He could see the silver-polish on the rails where the Shay had braked for the boulder on the tracks. He saw no sign of the boulder and he said so.

Marshal Bordon said, "Hell, that's easy, Longarm. They levered her over and let her roll down there in the dark. You'll never find her now, even if one boulder didn't look much like any other. The dry creekbed down there is paved with boulders, great and small."

As Longarm ran his fingers along the rail, Tom Carrol pointed up the slope. "They must have rolled her down from up yonder."

Another man said, "Tell us something we don't know, Tom. Anyone can see they had their pick. I can see a dozen rocks from here I could likely stop a train with."

Longarm hunkered over to run his hand along the other rail. The light was awful, but he could feel well enough in any light. Bordon asked him what on earth he was looking for.

"They didn't pry a rock loose and let her just roll," Longarm said. "The grassy scree up that way would be torn up if they'd rolled a big old rock down going lickety-split. It would have left sign hitting the track, too, and it didn't. I don't know where they got the rock, but it wasn't rolled on or off the tracks. It was *lifted.*"

"That's crazy!" Bordon said. The man who'd been on the train chimed in, "It's worse'n crazy, it's back-busting labor! I seen that rock and it was a big son of a bitch. If it was still here, it would come almost to your belt buckle, Longarm!"

Longarm started feeling the sun-bleached, splintered crossties he was hunkered on as he estimated how much a rock that tall had to weigh. He felt grit and held his fingers up to the meager light. "I'd say you're right. Did you notice what kind of rock it was, Pilgrim?"

"What kind of rock? Hell, it was *rock*-type rock, Longarm!"

"Think harder. There's rocks and then there's rocks. Was it granite, sandstone, shale, for God's sake, marble?"

"Hell, I ain't no mining man, Longarm. All rocks look like rocks to me."

"What color was it, then?"

"*Rock* color, damn it! It looked just like all the rocks you see this evening to every side. What are you driving at, Longarm?"

"I wish I knew. The country rock in this stretch is granite.

I'll take your word the rock that stopped the train must have been the same elephant gray, or you'd have noticed."

Longarm took an envelope from the pocket of his coat and put some pinches on the grit he'd found between the tracks in it. Then he picked up a lump of track ballast and put it in for luck. The railroad dick asked what he was up to.

Longarm straightened up and said, "The rock we're discussing left some grit on the ties it rested on. I mean to have an assay man look at it."

One of the other riders, who must have been a mining man, said, "Hell, granite don't shed if you treat it gentle, Longarm. You'd never bust up a granite boulder on a wood tie if you picked it up and put it there gentle."

"I know," said Longarm. "There's a chance the grit's from rail ballast. If it is, it'll match the lump I just seized as evidence. If it ain't, I'll have a better notion what sort of rock those fool owlhoots seem to be keeping as a pet."

Marshal Bordon gasped, "A pet rock? Who in thunder ever heard of a pet rock, Longarm?"

"Nobody—yet. But, as crazy as it seems, it surely looks as if the boys who stopped the train this evening brought their own rock along and then carried it off with them. Meanwhile, am I supposed to be doing all the tracking up here, or do any of you know how to look for sign?"

Marshal Bordon looked sheepish. "Fan out and see can you find any hoofprints and such, boys." His deputies did, but Longarm noticed that the railroad dick, Carrol, just sat there looking puzzled.

Longarm mounted up again and said softly, "Hoofprints are what *horsies* leave, moving their little footsies as they *go* someplace."

Tom Carrol flushed. "Hell, Longarm, you won't find any trail this time."

"How do you know? Seems to me we just got here, Carrol."

"Damn it, Longarm, look at the hard rocky scree all

53

about. Then look at how dark it's getting. Besides, we *have* looked for hoofprints and such in broad daylight. The gang never leaves any."

"Do you know that for a fact, or did you and the boys give up after trying the first few times?"

"Don't hooraw me, damn it! We've hunted high and low for the sons of bitches long before you ever got here to tell us they have some spooky way of riding off across country with heavy loot and now waist-high boulders!"

The discussion ended when a man on foot far up the track called out wearily, "It's no use, damn it! It's like looking for footprints on a cobblestone street! I can't even find a hunk of scree that looks like it's been moved for a month of Sundays."

Longarm called out to the man who said he'd been aboard the train. "Can you show us just which of the boulders up the slope the owlhoots popped from behind?"

"Not hardly," the other called back. "Look at how many of them there is!"

Longarm said he'd try that. He rode Copper upslope to the nearest good-sized granite boulder and dismounted again. He hunkered behind the rock, feeling the dirt with his fingertips as he tried to hide himself from view of the tracks. He didn't dig up anything more interesting than dust with his fingers and he couldn't get all of himself behind the boulder. Allowing for the fact he was bigger than some and that the crew and passengers might not have been paying attention, he still didn't think he'd have hidden behind this particular boulder. So, leading the patient Copper by the reins, he looked for better rocks to hide behind. He found a couple he could just about see using. But if anyone somewhat smaller than himself had used them, they'd left no traces.

He turned to remount. Then he spied something from the corner of his eye and moved over to pick it up. It was a cigarette end. Tailor-made. He sniffed and could tell it was Turkish tobacco. Hardly anyone he knew, save for women and sort of prissy men, smoked tailor-made Turkish cigarettes. Whoever had done so could not have thrown it up here from a passing train. It had been smoked down and dropped by someone standing—or, more likely, crouching—up here above the tracks. He put it away for safe keeping.

Now all he had to do was find a gent who smoked prissy cigarettes and lifted enormous rocks.

Chapter 5

He didn't mention his find when he rejoined the others at
trackside and agreed that they might as well call it a night.
As they headed back to town, Longarm fished out a cheroot
and lit up. As he'd expected, some of the other riders did
the same. He smelled cut plug, durham, Indian cured, and
worse, but nobody in the party seemed to fancy cigarettes,
Turkish or otherwise.

That didn't mean a hell of a lot. Birds of a feather didn't
have to smoke together, and he already knew the gents he
was riding with had been down in Peacock at the time of
the robbery.

Tom Carrol fell in beside him as they were riding back
through the tunnel. "I've been thinking about that odd business with your rock, Longarm."

"It ain't my rock. It's the Timberliners'."

"Whatever. The point is that more than one old boy has
allowed the Timberliners may be using some sort of vehicle
to move up and down the tracks without leaving a trail. If
a man had a rail car handy, it might not be too much work
to haul a rock along, right?"

Longarm shrugged. "I've been studying that. Where
would they have turned off the main line after the holdup?
They never went up the tracks past the passenger and crew.

They sure as hell didn't ride into town on wheels, with or without any rocks. Have you noticed any switches or sidings along this single-line track that I could have missed?"

"Well, no. But, damn it, they have to be getting away aboard *some* damn thing! How far could they get on foot with the heavy sacks of horn silver?"

"Not far, Tom. It gets sillier when you consider them carrying rocks along."

"All right. If they rode out mounted, by now someone surely would have found at least a trace of steel on rock. A man can amble over granite scree without leaving sign, but no horse or mule can."

"I've noticed that, Tom. Your notion of a handcar would work fine if you could tell me how they run it off the tracks after putting some distance between them and their victims."

Carrol shook his head. "I can't. It's a pure mystery. I have to confess the Timberliners have me confused total."

Longarm took a drag on his cheroot and said, "Don't worry about it, then. Uncle Sam already knowed you boys were confused. That's why they sent me up here to dis-confuse the situation."

"Jesus, Longarm, have you figured out what's going on already?"

"Nope. But, what the hell, I just got here."

It was standard practice in mining towns for the management class to dwell at a higher level than the common herd. So Marshal Bordon's frame house was up the slope west of town. Longarm thought that was dumb. The marshal had a haughty view of the rooftops along the main street, but since his house was even closer to the smoky overcast of Peacock, no matter which way a man aimed his nose, it smelled awful.

After bedding Copper with the marshal's pinto in the stable out back, Longarm went in with Bordon and met the family for supper. The marshal's wife was a tolerable-looking gal of forty-odd. She and her older husband had twin teenaged daughters named Susan and Sarah.

Supper was like the womenfolk of the household, simple but adequate. Mrs. Bordon served sausage and beans with cabbage. The two daughters fussed over him more than Longarm would have approved if he'd been their father. But neither the marshal nor his wife seemed to notice when young Susan—or was it Sarah?—shoved her cupcakes against the nape of Longarm's neck while reaching over his shoulder to pour him more coffee. It didn't matter which one had started acting sassy, since the other one nearly wound up in his lap as she served him apple pie. The attention, of course, had some effect on Longarm's glands, but not as much as they seemed to be trying for. He'd had a full-grown woman less than twenty-four hours back, and he knew the girls were just funning.

It wouldn't have been fair to say that the Bordon twins weren't as handsome as old Ruby, since they had youth and innocence as well as trim figures and pretty features going for them. But it was easy enough to resist temptation when he considered they were both likely virgins and that their daddy wore a .45 to the table.

Mrs. Bordon, who wore that same brown hair the same simple way and could have passed for the twins' older and wiser sister, said something about extra quilts for the bed in the guest room and both daughters jumped up, saying they'd be proud to make Longarm comfortable for the night.

Longarm smiled and said, "Hold on, ladies. I thank you all for the invite, but I'd best not stay here. You see, I'll be coming and going at odd hours. I have all sorts of things to check out, and I wouldn't want to wake the house prowling in and out like an alley cat."

The girls looked crestfallen. Marshal Bordon said, "Hell, that's no problem, Longarm. We can bed you in the tack room of the stable out back."

His wife clapped her hands. "Of course! Girls, fetch some bedding and make our guest a pallet in the tack room." She turned to Longarm and added, "You'll have your own private entrance and can come and go as you like."

The marshal laughed and said the outhouse was between

his back door and the stable, so that would be private, too. His wife lowered her eyes and blushed. Longarm could see that she was more refined than her husband.

More sober, too. Longarm had noticed that Bordon favored malt liquor over coffee with his supper, and though it was still early, he'd be three sheets to the wind by bedtime if he kept on drinking the way he was.

As Mr. Bordon cleared the table and the twins prepared his quarters, Longarm smoked and jawed some more with Bordon about the train robberies. But they were just going over the same ground. Bordon was a small-town lawman who would have had enough on his plate if the Timberliners had been half as slick.

Longarm asked if Tom Carrol was all there was to the railroad lines' security system.

Bordon said, "Nope. Tom has guards under him, riding the trains. Ned Durler—the old boy who rode out with us earlier—works for Tom as a riding dick. But Tom don't ride the trains his own self. He's just in charge. His office is in the roundhouse across the yards. Why?"

Longarm said he was just asking. He saw no sense in questioning the stupid railroad dick again so soon. It was still early and hopefully more serious gents might still be up and about along the short main street.

The twins came back in to say that his bed was fixed up in the tack room. Longarm got up. Bordon started to, looked sort of confused, and sat down again, almost missing his chair.

"You just set and keep Mrs. Bordon company, Marshal," said Longarm. "The gals can show me the way."

As Longarm followed the twins out the back door, he heard Mrs. Bordon calling her man an old fool. He pretended not to hear. The twins did, too. They were likely used to it. Longarm felt sort of sorry for all three of the females. Bordon was a nice enough old bird, but he couldn't have been too interesting to have about the house, even cold sober. It was easy enough to see why he and his family were stuck up here in the high country. They wouldn't have hired Bordon as a foot patrolman in Denver or even Dodge.

There wasn't all that much to praise about the way the twins had fixed up a sleeping pallet in one corner of the tack room, but Longarm praised it anyway. His bed was on the dirt floor behind the saddle racks and the place smelled like horse sweat and oiled harness leather. But, in truth, it could have been worse. He saw that the one door could be barred on the inside and the pallet in the corner was out of the line of fire from the one small window by the door. Then Susan—or maybe Sarah—spoiled it some by moving a vertical plank at one end of the tack room and explaining, "If you want to visit your horse you don't have to step outside. This is our secret passage."

Longarm said he hardly ever petted horses in the middle of the night and made a mental note that half the children in the neighborhood and likely some of their parents knew the fool twins had a loose board to play secret passage with. On the other hand, he knew where it was and he hoped the Timberliners were out-of-towners, who didn't even know where he meant to spend the night. He smiled at the twins and said, "I'm swearing you gals to another secret. I'm going down into town to look it over. I don't mean to tell anyone where I'm bedded down. So I sure hope you don't gossip much."

They laughed and said mum was the word, as though they'd found a new game—which they had, in a way. As Longarm walked outside, a twin fell in on either side, hanging on to his elbows. It felt sort of cozy, but Longarm tried not to think of the sassy twin sisters he'd once met on a riverboat with confusing—albeit delightsome—results. These twins were younger. And, drunk or sober, their pappy packed a .45.

They got out to the walk running downslope to the main street and Longarm paused to get his bearings. The two big streets of Peacock formed a cross like the sticks of a kite. The longer stick ran along the bottom of the valley with the railyards and the dry creekbed on the far side. The cross-stick street ran uphill each way. The marshal's house was halfway up the slope. When he asked the Bordon gals about the other houses strung along the cross-stick they said, as he'd suspected, that the doctors, lawyers, mine managers, merchants, and such lived up on this slope. The frame houses running up the far slope to the east were inhabited by foremen, railroad workers, barkeeps, and other lesser lights. Saloon swampers and common miners lived down along the south end of the longer main street. It wasn't a main street past the smelters farting sulfur smoke at the sky down that way.

He thanked them and pried himself loose to go exploring. As he walked down the hill he spied other families eating supper in the private homes along the plank walk. He'd thought the Bordons started a mite early. Old Marshal Bordon likely needed a head start, since he apparently waited till suppertime to do his drinking.

Longarm put Bordon's personal habits out of his mind. He hadn't come up here to pass judgement on anyone who wasn't messing with the U. S. mail, and it could have been worse. At least Bordon seemed sober enough on the job. He just wasn't very good at it.

Billy Vail had mentioned other federal men from the Post Office Department. Longarm had left Denver too quickly to go into it much. But now that he was here, he headed for the post office. The post office was in the back of a big hardware store on the main street, but the place seemed to be closed for the night. Longarm banged on the door and got no answer. The merchant-postmaster was likely having supper at his own house up the hill. It could wait until morning.

Longarm passed a barber shop and a couple of saloons still open. He didn't need a haircut and hardly anyone ever told him much about owlhoots in a small-town saloon. If there'd been any accurate local gossip about the Timberliners in these parts, the rascals would have been caught by now. Longarm knew he wasn't the first lawman, or even the first federal lawman, to take an interest in their mysterious career. Vail had said a couple of postal dicks had been gunned or were missing. He'd worry about that when he talked to the postmaster. It stood to reason he wasn't about to get much information out of a dead or missing post office dick.

The boardwalk under his boots began to tingle as he neared the impressive black mass of the stamping and smelter plant looming down where the street lamps started to peter out. He glanced to his left to see how the railroad felt about all this. But the light was awful and he had to take it on faith that they got the refined metal down to Tolland and the D&RG Western main line some way. None of the robberies had taken place south of Peacock, in any case.

He almost passed a small shop window with sedate gold letters across the glass when he noticed there was a light inside and that the lettering read, ASSAY OFFICE. CALVIN THAYER, PROP. So he opened the door and went in. The bell over the door brought a white-haired old gent out from the back room. "I was just fixing to close, cowboy," he said.

Longarm said, "I ain't a cowboy, I'm a deputy U. S. marshal and I sure hope you can stay open long enough to have a gander at some rock grit for me." He took out the envelope of whatever he'd found at the site of the last holdup and handed it to Thayer.

"Come on in the back, then," the assayer said. "What sort of ore do you figure you found?"

"I don't know as it's an ore sample. It may be scrapings from a rock."

Longarm explained the situation as they entered a workroom cluttered with work benches, dry sinks, and racks of chemicals all about. Thayer spilled the contents of the envelope onto a metal tray near a microscope and a jeweler's balance.

"I can tell you right off what this big lump is," he said. "It's trap rock. Railroad ballast. They quarried it up by Triple Tits."

Longarm frowned as he ran his mental map of the Amalgamated Railroad through his mind for such a settlement. "They told me the narrow-gauge runs from Peacock to Trinippy via Hanging Rock, Black Butte, Pipestone, and Lost Hat."

Thayer laughed. "The post office made the boys change the name of Triple Tits to something that'd look more sedate on the envelopes. So they named her Trinippy, but folks up here still call the end of the line Triple Tits. You see, there's these three big rounded peaks that look like big old tits, and—"

"I got it placed now. They look the same as you cross over the Divide west of Ward. By the way, is there any way to hook up by rail with the mining complex around Ward and Jamestown, farther up in Boulder County?"

Thayer shook his head as he prepared a slide to have a closer look at the grit from the envelope. "Triple Tits's way above timberline and well this side of Sawtooth Mountain. You could mayhaps ride a horse downslope and northeast to Jimtown. It'd be impossible to run rails that way."

"How wide a gap of rough country might there be between Triple Tits and the mining camps to the north?"

"It ain't the distance, it's the steep. A crow could make it from Triple Tits to Jimtown flying mayhaps twenty-odd miles. But neither man, beast, nor railroad locomotive comes with wings."

He crumpled the empty envelope in a ball, spread it on the table, and explained, "That's the lay of the land north of Triple Tits. Something awesome happened to the Rockies up near Cameron Pass a few million years back. Sawtooth Mountain, above the pass, is only the *biggest* peak that wound up sharp and jagged. Like I said, a man could ride or walk from Triple Tits down to tree-covered country, but not without hairpinning for miles of mighty rough country. Let's see what this grit is."

Longarm stood silent as the older man adjusted his microscope. "Hell, Deputy, this grit is just plain grit," he said at last. "I make out crystals of mica, feldspar, hornblend, and quartz. In other words, common country rock. There ain't a trace of color in it."

"You mean it's granite dust?"

"Sure. What did you figure the spine of the Rockies was made of? Cow shit?"

"It seemed sort of fine-grained to me, Mr. Thayer. Would you expect to scrape such fine-grained dust off a granite boulder, just banging it with a steel rail or perhaps other rocks?"

Thayer had another look, straightened up, and said, "It does look sort of powdery. It could be mine tailings."

"Say again?"

"You know, rock run through a stamp mill and treated to leach out any metals. Hold on a second. That's easy to check."

Longarm watched with interest as the assayer put a pinch of grit in a test tube and dropped some reagent in on the sample with a glass pipette. Thayer swished the mess around, holding the test tube to the light.

"Sure, that's what the stuff is," he said. "Mine tailings. You find piles of the shit all up and down the line. Every mine on the narrow-gauge high grades its ore before shipping it down her to the smelters. What we got here is the coffee grounds of somebody's silver mine."

"Is there any silver in that dust?"

"Not enough to detect easily. But there's chlorine traces left by the leaching process. I'd say this stuff was never scraped off any boulder of country rock. It's just dust blown off someone's tailings dump."

"How would it wind up along a stretch of clear open track with no mine close enough to mention?"

"Haven't you ever heard of the wind, son? It's calm up here tonight, but when the Chinook's pouring over the Divide, you'll see more than fine dust blowing up and down the valley. I'm sorry, deputy, but this shit ain't no clue. It's just common, worthless dirt."

Longarm said, "Sometimes no clue can be a clue. If what you say is true, those train robbers moved a rock that must have weighed tons on and off the railbed without leaving a trace."

Thayer shrugged. "I heard about the robbery this evening. It seems to me you're making a mountain out of a boulder, son. They rolled her down on the tracks from above, stopped the train, then levered her over the far side to let her roll on down to join the others in the dry creek. They might have managed to do so without scratching up the rails. Or you might have missed the marks in the poor light. What difference does it make? No man with a lick of sense packs a private boulder about with him when there are hundreds of thousands of the fool things all along the roadbed on both sides. It ain't like there's a shortage of rocks in the Rockies, you know."

Longarm thanked him and left, feeling sort of foolish. Thayer's words made sense. Longarm had caught himself looking for complicated answers to simple questions on other occasions. It hurt to think that he might have misread sign, up the line. But he was damned if he could see any reason for a serious gang of owlhoots to pack a private boulder about with them, even if they had a handcar they were using, which he doubted.

Thinking about wheeled vehicles made Longarm cross the dusty street and find a cinder path toward the railroad yards. It was dark once he got away from the main street, but when he found the place where he'd stopped the runaway locomotive, he saw that they'd levered her back onto the tracks and rolled her away somewhere for the night. He saw lights in the window of the little red schoolhouse he'd saved, so he went over to see what was going on.

It sounded like a fight inside as he mounted the wooden steps. Some gal was yelling, "Out, damned spot!" at the top of her lungs. Longarm drew his .44 and opened the door to save her.

Everyone inside stopped yelling as he burst in. He smiled sheepishly and holstered his gun as he saw that he'd walked in on a mess of folks practicing some sort of theatrics. The men and women using one end of the school as an improvised stage were dressed normally, but one bald gent in a snuff-colored suit was holding a tin sword and the fat lady who'd been yelling about her spots had a gilt paper crown on. A younger and handsomer gal in a gingham smock called out, "Gaylord, we were so worried about you! Where have you been all this time?"

Then, as Longarm moved into the light, she blinked in surprise. "Oh, *you're* not Gaylord Jones!"

Longarm said, "No, ma'am, I'm Custis Long, and I work for the Justice Department. Ain't you the lady who was on the porch when I rode that Shay locomotive almost to your door this evening?"

She gasped. "Oh, you must be the lawman who saved our school! I'm Beth Simmons, the teacher, and I've been meaning to look you up and thank you, Marshal Long."

"Just doing my job, ma'am. Could I ask what's going on here, and why you thought I could possibly be connected with it?"

The pretty brunette schoolmarm dimpled as she explained, "This is the Peacock Drama Club. We're rehearsing *Macbeth,* for we mean to stage it next week for the town. We've been waiting and waiting for a professional actor and drama coach to arrive. For a moment, in the dim light, I thought you were he."

"How come, ma'am? I hardly ever go to plays, let alone act in them."

"I can see that," she laughed. "But you're about the same height and build as Gaylord Jones, and since we've been expecting him for days..."

"Oh, I see the light now, ma'am. I'm sorry I ain't an actor. But—hold on a minute. You say this actor gent, about my size and build, was due here before I arrived? Could he have got off the D&RG Western sometime the day before yesterday?"

"That's when he wired he'd arrive. Why do you ask? Have you seen him?"

"Not hardly, but it's starting to look like somebody else might have. Could somebody tell me where the Western Union office is in town?"

66

The man packing the tin sword said that Longarm could send a wire to Denver from the office across from the round-house and open-shed depot. So Longarm thanked them all and lit out before he had to tell them he suspected that the acting coach they were expecting didn't figure to arrive.

He still wasn't sure. He, and doubtless Billy Vail, had been puzzled by the man shot in Longarm's place not having any papers on his body. It was possible some townie in Tolland had helped himself to the dead man's wallet. But the body had arrived in Denver with a gun on one hip, a gold watch, and loose change in one pocket.

He found the telegraph office and sent a night letter to his boss, assuring Vail that he'd finally arrived where he'd been sent and bringing Denver up on the case to date. He chewed the end of his pencil stub as he thought of some things he wanted to have checked out. There were lots of questions, but they refused to fall into a sensible pattern. He wrote the name of the missing actor and suggested they have someone check the body in the Denver morgue out with somebody who knew the rascal. Somebody in Denver had to know the features of a touring actor, if he was real. Meanwhile, who'd ever heard of an actor wandering about without a scrapbook, let alone some identification?

He made a mental note to talk some more about him with that pretty Beth Simmons, sometime when he found her alone. He didn't want the whole town jawing about someone murdering Gaylord Jones until he was sure the man was dead. And there was still an outside chance that the killers didn't know they'd gunned the wrong man yet. Everyone in Peacock knew that Longarm had arrived safe and sound. But no trains had left for the higher country to the north since he'd arrived. So if the Timberliners were based somewhere out in the hills, they deserved no favors.

There was a light in the roundhouse next door. Longarm didn't go there. He knew that neither the locomotives nor Tom Carrol, if he was there, could tell him much he didn't already know.

He consulted his watch. The night was young. The mills stayed open all night, in any case. So he ambled down to talk to the mill hands about their work.

Chapter 6

Talking in a stamping mill wasn't easy, even when the night foreman led him into a cubbyhole office and shut the door. The foreman was an old-timer with a grizzled beard and a drinker's nose, but he seemed to know his oats. He agreed with the assayer, Thayer, that finding mine tailings on the roadbed of a mining railroad was no mystery. He said there was no place to turn off the main line aboard a handcart between where they were and the scene of the holdup. He said the nearest mine adit was a quarter of a mile down the vale, toward Tolland. So, in the first place, anyone riding away from the scene of the crime, with or without a pet rock, would have preceded Longarm and the runaway Shay through Peacock. And, in the second place, that old mine was abandoned and boarded up, and the old tracks in and out of it had long ago been salvaged.

Longarm asked if it had been a copper mine.

The foreman nodded. "It was. How did you know?"

"Name of your town. Peacock ore is found in copper mines."

"You sounded like a gent who's passed through the high country afore. Yeah, the Peacock was the first mine in these parts. Some of her copper went into the transcontinental telegraph lines. But that was a long time ago, son. The copper combine bottomed out and this town was fixing to go ghost when Lucky Larson found silver chloride farther up the vale. It saved the town, what there is of her. The smelters, stores, and such were already here. So they just run the rails on up to the silver lodes to the north."

"I know about them. Let's talk about the old Peacock copper mine."

"Hell, son, we just did. You can go down the vale and look her over any time you like. There's nobody guarding an empty hole in the ground."

"Is she a big mine?"

"Used to be before she caved in. You can't get in more'n a hundred feet from the adit, and that ain't safe. When they abandoned her, they salvaged the timbers as well as the tracks, so the mountain's sort of settled in. The stamping you can feel with your boots has a way of caving in untimbered drifts, you see."

"I noticed that the ground sort of shakes in these parts. Did you or any of your crew ever work in the old Peacock mine?"

"Nope. Like I said, it bottomed out years ago. I could get you a chart of the old works, if you want one, too."

"I'd like that. What do you mean, too? Has someone else asked to see the old blueprints?"

"Yep. Post office dick, a week or so ago. I told him the company might have the old abandoned shafts charted, if only to keep from drilling into one underground. Nobody likes surprises. He said he'd send for them his own self. So I never."

Longarm frowned as he took out two cheroots, offered one to the helpful foreman, and said he'd sure like to see the layout of the old mine to the south. The foreman said it would take a day or so, since the main office was in Denver. He added, "The deserted shafts are all caved in but, like I said, it can be a mortal surprise drilling into gas-filled goat. Are you figuring on starting your own mine?"

"Not hardly. Let me ask you another question. Does one

70

mining company run all the shafts up the line?"

"Not exactly. My company owns the narrow-gauge, this town, and the milling operation. The mines up the line at Hanging Rock, Pipestone, Lost Hat, and Triple Tits are owned and operated private, but sort of tied in with the Amalgamated Company as a loose syndicate."

"I see. That's why it's called amalgamated. But you missed a mine. Who digs silver at Black Butte?"

"Nobody. It's Amalgamated property. We get our coal and trap rock from Black Butte. Ain't no color along that stretch."

"I see. Someone said one mine at least produced gold as well as silver."

"That's Triple Tits, at the end of the line. They've found a little native gold threaded through the silver chloride beds up yonder. Not enough to pay if they wasn't digging rich silver as well."

Longarm blew a thoughtful smoke ring.

The foreman asked, "Don't you want to know about horn silver, like that post office gent?"

"What did he ask? And, while we're talking about him, what happened to him?"

The foreman shrugged and said, "Nobody knows."

"Let's talk about horn silver, then," Longarm said. "Is ore that rich worth packing out of the high country in a sack?"

"I'd say she was a break-even proposition. Horn is nigh pure silver, but silver prices is down to where you got to carry fifteen pounds of pure silver to add up to a pound of gold. A man could mayhaps pack a few hundred dollars at a time in his saddlebags. I reckon it beats honest work, but it's still tedious when you throws in the risk. You ain't the first lawman who's followed this particular notion. I'm no detective, but I'd say there has to be a more sensible way for them Timberliners to fence their loot."

"How come? Seems to me many an owlhoot would rather pack a few hundred dollars' worth of horn silver out of the

71

mountains than string fences or herd cows. Say he took a week getting back to civilization. It still adds up to handsome day wages."

The old foreman shook his head. "It won't work. Them holdup men has been stealing *horn* silver, not *sterling* silver. You can't sell even a pretty ore on the silver market till it's been refined. So them rascals has to have a refinery, see?"

Longarm nodded. Before he could ask, the foreman said, "They ain't been refining horn silver here. We'd have noticed. There ain't no other mills in Colorado refining ore for mysterious strangers, neither. Them post office dicks already checked that out afore the Timberliners got 'em."

Longarm blew another smoke ring. "No offense, but would it be possible for you to get me the work sheets on just who's been running what through your mills?"

The foreman opened a rolltop desk and took out a sheaf of onion-skin flimsies. "I've been expecting someone to act smart," he said. "So you can keep these carbon copies. "You'll see that, save for the horn silver and gold dust stopped afore it ever got here, we've been processing exactly what the mines has shipped us. No more, no less. When we get enough ingots together to send down the narrowgauge to Tolland, it goes under heavy guard, and nobody's ever tried to stop it. If you can find a hundred ounces of pure we can't account for, I'll eat this smelter with the fires going!"

Longarm thanked him and put the onion skins away to read later. Then he left the old timer an extra cheroot and said adios for now.

He headed back for Marshal Bordon's house on the hill. He was running out of other places to look at in the dark. He was in the dark in more ways than one. He could see where he was walking, but nothing else made a lick of sense.

The Timberliners, whoever they might be, were not running a regular train-robbing operation. Not unless they were all completely loco. They had some neat tricks for stopping trains and getting away clean in open country. But that was where it started going crazy. They hadn't made one attempt on the riches of the bigger D&RG main line just to the south. They hadn't even helped themselves to the pure bullion traveling narrow-gauge down to the main line.

He muttered, "Somebody's high grading." But that didn't work so good, either. If the owners of one mine were helping themselves to the cream of their neighbors' ore shipments down the mountain, it would show on the records of the mills. Or would it? Longarm groaned aloud as he considered the legwork that suspicion led to. He'd hold off on that notion until he had had a chance to study the papers. Catching crooks on paper was tedious as hell and hard to prove. Even if one particular mine was showing unusual profits at the moment, he'd have nothing he could accuse them of save American enterprise. He had to catch some son of a bitch with stolen horn silver on him. After that, it hardly mattered where the hell he was taking it.

Longarm knew that while at least one or more of the gang were killers, the others weren't. They hadn't treated their victims all that inconsiderately. If he nabbed one, and pointed out the advantages to his neck of turning state's evidence, a lot of these infernal loose ends would just get explained the easy way.

Longarm stiffened and broke stride as something darted across his path in the gloom. So whoever had been leading him with a rifle sight from the darkness to his right missed Longarm's head—just—to pluck the cheroot from his mouth with whizzing hot lead.

By the time the rifle fired a second time, Longarm had hit the grit and rolled, grabbing for his own hardware. The second shot went over him high. He fired at the muzzle flash and kept rolling. The third shot blew a gout of cinder dust out of the spot he'd just vacated. This time, Longarm aimed seriously and had the satisfaction of hearing his round thunk into something solid as he kept rolling. He got himself behind a pile of trackside trash. A bullet hit it from the less friendly side. So he knew his attacker was either still up and able, or backed by at least one friend. This situation was getting downright mean.

Longarm knew he was outlined by the street lighting behind him, while the only way he could get an educated shot at the other side was whenever they fired directly at him.

But he spied no further muzzle flashes. He heard lots of running footsteps. Some running his way and others, out in the dark yards, going the other. He rolled on one elbow to look toward the more civilized parts of town and saw that half of it was headed his way, excited. A couple of the townsmen were packing lanterns. As soon as he saw that nobody from the inky black yards seemed to be interested in shooting anyone but him, Longarm called out, "Toss one of the oil lamps out across the tracks and let's have some light on the subject, boys!"

A man dressed railroad and packing a cheap lantern wound up and threw it like a ball. It sailed out into the darkness and exploded on the tracks. Longarm said, "There you go. I owe you a drink."

But as he rose to one knee, his .44 looking the same way, he saw nothing out there but railroad tracks lying flat in the flickering orange light. He knew he hadn't hit anyone serious and, as they had to be out of range from him by now, Longarm got all the way up, dusting off his duds with his hat while he held his muzzle down.

The nice young railroader who'd thrown the lantern asked him what was going on, adding that they'd heard a mess of shots. Longarm put his hat back on and started to reload. "You heard me and at least one Winchester .44-40," he said. "I'll never say a black cat means bad luck again, for one just saved my life. I was fired on from the dark yonder."

A couple of Marshal Bordon's town deputies stepped out of the growing crowd to fan out across the tracks. One had a lantern. Longarm didn't see the marshal himself. He hadn't expected to. But Tom Carrol came up to him, asking what had happened.

"I've just told everyone and it's getting tedious,"

Longarm said. "Where were you just now, Tom?"

Carrol pointed back the way Longarm had come. "In my office at the roundhouse, of course. How many of them were there, Longarm?"

"Don't know. Couldn't see 'em. I suspicion I hit one. But the son of a bitch must have run off winged. How many doctors do you have here in Peacock?"

"Only one. Doc Forbes, up the slope to the west. He works outten his own house. Why?"

"We'd best stake the doc out. A man don't wander far with a .44 slug in him, even as a flesh wound. If I hit the rascal anywhere, he's bound to consider medical attention once the shock wears off."

The railroad dick snapped his fingers. "Hot damn! It gets even better once you study on it! If we know the man who tried to gun you has a round in him, we can safely say anyone who don't can't be him, right!"

"Up to a point. If there were two of them, it only works halfway."

"Yeah, but there ain't that many boys up here in the vale, even when you count the other camps. I'll get my railroad guards to ask all along the line and if anyone's wounded, or even just missing..."

One of the town deputies came back, holding something in his palm. "Found a spent .44-40, like you guessed, Longarm," he said.

"I wasn't guessing," the lawman replied. "I pack a .44-40 Winchester on my own saddle. And so does just about everyone else, damn it."

"Yeah, them gents gunned just south of town was hit with the same kind of rounds, too. Life would be simpler if the killer used something fancier. But eight out of ten saddle guns west of the Big Muddy are .44-40 Winchesters."

Tom Carrol said, "A Remington or Henry would fire the same Winchester rounds, wouldn't they, boys?"

Longarm shook his head. "They would, but they'd sound a mite different coming out of another gun. The son of a bitch didn't just fire once at me. I'm sort of used to the

75

sound. But let's not pick infernal nits. Let's start looking for some son of a bitch with one of my balls in him, and it won't matter what he was trying to gun me with."

Chapter 7

Longarm and the boys crowded into the nearest saloon: the boys to celebrate his narrow escape, Longarm to count noses. He didn't know half the folks in Peacock, of course, but by discreet questioning he was able to establish that nobody one would usually find up and about at this hour was missing, and of course he'd have noticed if anyone in the crowd had been bleeding enough to matter.

The older, married Peacockers tended to spend their evenings at home with their families. That meant that more than half the gents in town had to be taken on trust. On the other hand, since womenfolk tended to ask all sorts of fool questions about a man's comings and goings, Longarm hadn't met many train robbers who lived at home regular. They said Jesse James, wherever he was these days, lived quietly when he was home with his wife and kin. He did his train robbing when he was off on what he told his wife and the neighbors was a horse-trading expedition. But Longarm didn't suspect the James-Younger gang of being the Timberliners. The Timberliners weren't acting that sensibly.

Longarm knew that any professionals would have moved on by now. The pickings up here were slim, and anyone could see that the U. S. government as well as two county sheriffs were taking a mighty personal interest in this business.

Longarm went easy on the beer, aware that he was a mile higher than his usual haunts along Larimer Street. Some of the others didn't seem to care if they got drunk or not. Getting drunk seemed to be one of the only entertainments in these mining towns. The gent he'd seen waving a toy sword around over at the schoolhouse had joined the party, without the sword. He turned out to be the postmaster, who also ran the hardware store.

Longarm bought him a drink. The part-time actor, part-time postmaster, and serious dealer in hardware and mining supplies was named Albert Wrenn. He said it was all right to call him Al, so Longarm did. Al backed up what they'd told Longarm at the mills about the post office dicks arriving earlier and either getting shot or vanishing. Al said he had no idea what else was going on.

Longarm smiled crookedly. "I admire a man who don't flap his jaw when he has nothing to say, Al. It seems that everyone else in this crowd has his own solution to the mystery, and none of 'em works."

Wrenn nodded and replied, "I don't have to offer helpful suggestions. I got me an alibi for every damned time the Timberliners has hit."

"Do tell? I disremember asking you for alibis, Al."

"I know your reputation, Longarm. Sooner or later, you'll wind up checking out everyone in town. So I'll save you the trouble. I run the store and the post office six days a week and I acts as a sexton in the church on Sundays. As you saw at the schoolhouse, earlier, I spend most of my free time after hours with the drama club. Miss Beth Simmons says I got a natural talent for acting. I'm playing Macduff next week, if that fool Gaylord Jones ever shows up to be Macbeth so's I can sword-fight with him. We generally finish at the schoolhouse about nine or ten. I left early tonight when I heard all the gunplay. Do you want to meet up with the Arapaho squaw I keeps as a maid of all work at my house up the hill?"

"Not hardly, Al. In the first place, Uncle Sam disapproves of cohabitation with tribal Indians, so the less I know the better. In the second place, we both know not one train's been robbed late at night. Mainly 'cause they don't run the trains at night."

"There you go, then. Don't it feel grand to have one man in town you can trust? You know, of course, the robberies have to be inside jobs."

Al said that as a statement, not a question. Longarm took a sip of beer and asked, "What makes you say that, Al?"

The Peacocker snorted. "Hell, it's obvious. There's nobody camped out in the open above timberline between jobs. A dozen posses has gone over the high range, looking, and never found so much as a campfire site. It gets *cold* up there at night, Longarm. Them outlaws have to hole up indoors between jobs. And, afore you ask, there ain't no ghost camps or abandoned cabins close enough to matter. Besides, that missing post office dick told me. He said the gang had to know when the trains was rolling and, more important, what was on 'em. The gang has yet to hit a work train or a train just carrying low grade down here to the mills. He said something about talking to the mine supers up the line, just afore he rode off into nowheres. It stands to reason he was on to something."

Longarm pursed his lips as he ran over his mental list of earlier arrivals. He said, "The post office men who were bushwhacked and found are accounted for. The missing gent was Postal Inspector Crawford, right?"

"Yep. He was jawing with me, over to my post office, just afore he vanished."

"What did he look like, Al?"

"Say again? What difference do it make what he looked like?"

"Might help if I ever stumble over him, dead or otherwise."

"Hell, he's been looked for. But, all right, he was a natural-looking gent, about thirty. Clean-shaved, with brown hair and eyes. He wore ordinary duds, and I disremember any scars or tattoos. By now he's likely a skeleton."

"How come? It's my understanding that he broke off contact with the post office just about the time they were asking for my help on the case. Exactly what day did he vanish?"

Wrenn thought and then shook his head with a puzzled frown. "I can't pin her down. You see, nobody was taking notes at the time, since we didn't know he was aiming to drop out of sight."

Longarm shook his head and said, "It had to be earlier this week. He'd already stopped answering wires from his home office when they told me to come up here and look for him and the gents who vanished him. Can't you pin the date down?"

"I'll study on it. Maybe some of the other boys will remember. He jawed some with others about town, so I'll start asking."

A railroader who'd been listening chimed in. "I know the gent you boys is talking about. He rode up to Hanging Rock with us—let's see, I reckon it might have been Saturday."

Al said, "Marshal Bordon would know. The post office wired him to look for Crawford when he stopped answering his mail."

They were still arguing about it as Longarm drifted away. Longarm was all too familiar with the fuzzy memories of witnesses. It was one of the problems all lawmen had to deal with. Naturally, nobody had noticed the nondescript post office dick until his whereabouts had become an item of local interest.

Longarm didn't have to ask why Al Wrenn figured he'd be skeletonized by now, no matter exactly when he'd dropped out of sight. Since the search parties hadn't found him, Crawford had been shoved down a hole or buried with rocks. During the short summers up here, the ants and pack rats had to work like hell storing food and fat for the long, hungry winter.

He put the missing man on the back burner for now.

Bordon would have the exact date, if it turned out to be important. No matter what had happened to the post office dick, he was in no position to help solve the case now, save perhaps as evidence.

That hardly seemed likely. The killer working for the Timberliners was acting downright inconsiderate by using untraceable, common ammo.

He was feeling the needle beer a mite when he left the saloon. He was tired of getting shot at, so he ducked up an alley and made sure he wasn't being trailed before he headed back to the Bordon house. When he arrived, the house was dark. He didn't want to jaw with the half-drunk old man, so he walked quietly to the stable and let himself into the tack room.

He barred the door and undressed in the dark. The tack room smelled stuffy, but he left the grimy window shut. It felt good to slip naked between the clean cotton sheets. He had to remember to go easy on that needle beer until his head adjusted to the altitude. He wasn't drunk, but he was sleepier than he usually felt at this hour. He tucked his gun between the pallet and the plank wall and rolled over to get some shuteye. He noticed, then, he had a hard on.

That was likely the altitude, too. He hadn't even been thinking about she-males since he'd left that handsome schoolmarm some time back. And, hell, who wanted to mess with a gal who spent all her free time with Shakespeare?

Longarm didn't remember dozing off, but he knew he must have when he woke up suddenly, aware that he was not alone on the pallet. He went for his gun with one hand as he rolled and pinned his invisible visitor down with his free hand and full weight.

A she-male voice gasped, "Stop! You're hurting me!"

Longarm reconsidered and didn't pistol whip whoever he'd pinned, after all. He noticed that whoever it was had a thin shift and right nice breasts positioned tightly against his bare chest. He asked, "What are you doing here, Susan? Or is it Sarah?"

She said, "I'm Susan. I didn't know if you were back yet. I couldn't find the lamp. I came to get my balls."

"Do tell? How old might you be, honey?"

"Going on sixteen. Why?"

"That's mighty young to be reaching for balls. I'd like to oblige you, but a man has to draw the limit somewhere! You'd best go back to your own bed and leave my balls alone."

"Silly, they're not your balls. They're *my* balls. Let me up and I'll show them to you."

He rolled off her and propped himself up on one elbow, muttering, "You surely talk confusing."

Susan struck a match. "See if you can spy the lamp."

Longarm just stared at her warily. The young gal was wearing no more than he'd suspected as she sat on her folded knees. Beyond her he saw where she'd slipped in by moving that secret plank. She reached past him to pull something from a slot between the planks of that wall, saying, *"Here* are my balls. I remembered after I went to bed that I'd left them here."

The match went out, but not before Longarm had seen the pair of egg-sized tinfoil balls she was after. He laughed weakly and said, "Oh, *them* kind of balls. I thought . . . never mind what I thought."

She said, "I have to be careful with my balls. Sarah steals them. I think I'll hide them in the sofa cushions in the sitting room for now. Don't you think that's a good idea?"

"I don't know. I don't hide tinfoil balls much. What's the point of this game you and your twin are playing?"

"Oh, you know, you save tinfoil from cigars and such, and after you have enough saved you can turn it in for money. Tin is right valuable."

He chuckled. "So I hear. I hate to spoil a dream, honey, but whoever started that notion about saving tinfoil must have had a mean streak. Tin ain't worth all that much. You'd have to save up a wagonload before anyone dealing in scrap metal would bother with you. That's why they use tinfoil for waterproof packaging. The stuff is cheap."

"How can that be, sir? I heard some miners saying that there isn't one tin mine in Colorado!"

"There ain't. Ain't a tin mine in North America, that I know of. But tin is still cheap. They import it from Singapore and South America at about the price of zinc. But never mind, you go on and save it all you want to. It can't hurt."

The thinly clad woman-child crouching innocently under the covers a few inches from his erection said, "Oh, pooh! I'll never in this world save up a wagonload. But let's not tell Sarah. I'll just put my balls back and let her steal them, and the joke will be on her. All right?"

"Mum's the word. Ah, don't you reckon you ought to study on going back to bed before your folks miss you, honey?"

"Ma and Pa are sleeping sound. But I'll go, if you promise not to tell Sarah about my balls."

"I swear I won't. I hardly ever discuss balls with fifteen-year-olds."

So she gave him a peck on the cheek and scampered off, leaving Longarm with a raging erection and considerable pride in his self-restraint.

He lay back down, cursing softly under his breath. Then he laughed at himself. It was a caution how quickly a man forgot. He'd thought, when he'd tiptoed out on Ruby in Salt Lake, that he wouldn't want a woman for at least a year.

Maybe that Beth Simmons at the schoolhouse could use an extra spear carrier or somebody that didn't have to say any funny words in her fool play. He knew that if she'd been in bed with him just now they wouldn't have been discussing the price of tin. Beth Simmons looked a mite prim, but a man wouldn't have to worry about her being under age. He figured she must be in her late twenties. By that age, if a gal put out at all, a man knew he wasn't getting no fool virgin who'd weep and wail about it in the cold gray dawn. On the other hand, Beth had looked very prim, despite the way she filled out her smock. But, hell, if she was a proper old maid, he wasn't going to get next to her at this late date, so what was he worried about?

He started to drop off again. Then he heard that same board creak and rolled up with a weary frown, asking, "Susan?"

A deeper she-male voice replied, "Heavens, what would either of my girls be doing here at this hour? I came to see if you were comfortable and if there was anything I could do to make you more so."

"Mrs. Bordon?"

"Call me Livia," she replied, sliding under the covers with him. As their hips touched, he could tell she wasn't even wearing a thin nightgown. She was bare-ass naked.

He said, "Well, far be it from me to refuse kind hospitality, ma'am. But are you sure your husband won't mind?"

"Don't tease me, Custis. You know full well the old man I married is dead drunk. He hasn't touched me for over a year—and a woman has needs!"

Longarm still might have resisted temptation had he had any say in the matter. But Livia Bordon wrapped her arms around him and kissed him hot and dirty, with her big warm breasts pressed against him as she cocked a naked thigh over his hip to press her apron of damp pubic hair against his lap. Since part of his lap was standing at full attention in the dark, he was halfway in her before he could chide her for her forward manners.

So he growled, "Oh, hell," with her lips pressed to his, and rolled her on her back to mount her right. She moaned in pleased surprise as he entered her to the roots and started posting in the saddle of her wide, welcoming thighs. She rolled her head from side to side as he nibbled her throat and just accepted what fate had provided. He knew he was going to feel rotten about this at breakfast, but he knew she'd never forgive him in any case, if he stopped now.

Livia moaned, "That's the biggest, nicest thing I've ever had in me!"

"Do you want to talk dirty or do you want to make love?" he asked.

She wrapped her legs around him, dug her nails into his back, and gasped, "I don't care if this is love or not. I just want more of it! Screw me, darling! Screw me hard and never stop!"

That was impossible, of course—but Longarm aimed to please. So when he ejaculated in her he kept moving enough to keep hard as he got his breath back.

She laughed. "Oh, you *are* a real man. But you're teasing me so. I'm right on the edge but I can't get there with you moving so slow and . . . forget what I just said!"

She started bumping up at him with her hips as he kept moving slowly and deliberately. If felt good, and she deserved to be punished. But it didn't seem to be hurting the cheating wife worth mention as she shuddered on his shaft in a long, luxurious orgasm. So, not wanting to let her have all the adulterous fun, Longarm commenced to pound her hard again. He did it for his own enjoyment, and his enjoyment was considerable. Livia hissed between her teeth and gasped, "Oh, my God, I'm coming againnnnn!"

That made two of them. It seemed there was no justice. Longarm went limp, still in the saddle, as Livia's internal muscles milked his semi-sated shaft. She murmured, "Oh, thank you, thank you. You've no idea how much I needed that."

He said, "You're wrong. I was there, too. But we'd best study on the way we've been carrying on, honey. I don't hold on sharing bedroom privileges with a man I've broken bread with."

"Pooh! I was the one who baked the bread! Is it my fault my husband is an old drunk?"

"Yes, ma'am, it is. You married up with him. I've avoided the trap myself, but I've been to many a wedding and I know the small print. There ain't nothing in the vows saying one foresakes all others unless there's a younger gent in the tack room on occasion."

She stiffened in his arms. "Are you moralizing at a time like this? Your cock is still *in* me, you fool!"

He grinned sheepishly and answered, "Damned if it ain't.

And if I had any character, I'd take it out."

She moved her pelvis skillfully as she asked, coyly, "Do you *want* to take it out, Custis?"

"Nope. Just said I ought to. It do feel like you've been sort of neglected down there and, what the hell, we've already sinned a mite. May as well sin right as long as we're about it."

So she rolled over and asked him to sin her dog style, praising the depths of his sinfulness at that angle, then climbing on top to let him rest while she sinned for both of them.

Chapter 8

At breakfast the next morning, Longarm managed to keep a sober face as he ate ham and eggs across the table from Marshal Bordon. The twins ate breakfast like the innocent maidens he hoped they were. But old Livia kept sneaking him winks and grinning—as she had every right to, when you studied on it.

He'd extracted a promise from her before she'd left that their one wild fling in the feathers was to be it. He hoped she meant to live up to it, for he'd likely be spending another night here and he knew his own weak nature. It was easy as hell to resist temptation, wide awake, fully dressed, and recently pleasured. He wasn't sure he could keep his head so level should a bawdy naked gal sneak up on him after a full day of keeping his pecker in his pants. He'd have to study on a safer place to bed down. There was no hotel in Peacock. If he stayed here, it was only a question of time before he got caught in bed with that older man's woman, and he didn't want to have a fight with old Bordon. The poor old gent had enough on his plate.

Bordon ate sparely, like a man with a hangover. They didn't talk much at table, and Longarm was glad. He hated talking two-faced, and he knew the small-town lawman didn't have any sensible ideas about the train robberies in any case.

As soon as it was decent, Longarm excused himself and left the Bordon house to amble down the hill. He went to the railyards, looked up the dispatcher, and asked when the next narrow-gauge was heading up the mountain. It turned out one was leaving within the hour. So Longarm bummed a seat and, while he waited, went over to the hardware store and post office.

Al Wrenn was behind the hardware counter, not the post-office window, but he said he'd open the post office if Longarm wanted to send a letter.

Longarm said, "I just thought up a question. The federal angle in this operation is the mail sacks they've scattered about on the tracks. Can you tell me if there's a post office like this up at the other mining camps I'm fixing to visit?"

Wrenn nodded. "Sure. This one's the biggest, though. Why?"

"Just asking. In other words, all the outbound letters interfered with have been stamped and postmarked, right?"

"Of course. But what's your point? The robbers have searched the mail sacks looking for gold pokes and horn silver. They haven't taken any of the letters themselves."

"Are you sure of that, Al?"

"Sure I'm sure. We naturally checked that right off. Asked the boys up the line, and none of them sent anything that didn't get through. Are you suggesting an ulterior motive in trifling with those mail sacks?"

"I was, but forget it. Happened on another mail case I worked one time that the crooks were trying to prevent certain news from reaching the outside world. But if the Timberliners ain't been stealing any letters.... Hold on. Can you say for sure not one letter's even been opened, Al?"

"Sure I can. After they were picked up from the rocks they all came here to be resorted and sent on. I'd have noticed had any been torn open. Like I said, the robbers just dumped the contents of the sacks, looking for precious metal. They never even asked for the valuables of the passengers and crew they held up at gunpoint."

Longarm said, "So I hear. It don't make sense. As I was saying just last night, once you sin, you may as well sin serious. Them Timberliners figure to spend a lot of time at hard for robbing anyone of anything. So why pass up a gold watch or fat wallet for a mess of crude silver?"

"Maybe they got a fence who can unload the horn silver but don't want to deal in more traceable loot."

"Hell, how can anyone trace money, Al?"

"Try her this way. The robberies have gone slick and sudden. Mayhaps the Timberliners don't want to waste time searching through people's pockets?"

Longarm took out a cheroot and lit it. "Maybe. Timing does seem important to the rascals. Do you stock tobacco here? I'd best pick up some smokes while I have the chance."

Wrenn said he didn't carry cheroots but that Longarm could get some a few doors down. Longarm thanked him and did so. As he bought a fistful of cheroots he asked the tobacco-shop man if he sold any fancy cigarettes. The shop keeper said he had some, somewhere in the back, but that he hadn't sold any in recent memory. "There's no demand for the sissy things. But I can dig 'em out for you if you have a minute."

Longarm said he didn't smoke like a sissy either and left, frowning. At least one of the Timberliners fancied tailor-made cigarettes, but he couldn't have bought them in Peacock. It would be interesting to ask if any had been sold at the other camp stores up the line.

He went to the Western Union office to see if Billy Vail had anything to say. Billy had wired him a night letter, but had nothing to say. The dead man in the Denver morgue lay still unknown. Vail was working on the odds on him being Gaylord Jones, the actor. He said he'd never heard of him.

That was something to study on, too. Billy and Mrs. Vail went to all the shows in Denver, even the fool opera. He'd have to jaw some more with the schoolmarm about her drama coach when he got back.

Longarm mounted to the cab to ride the northbound narrow-gauge. He wanted to have a better look at the country and the dispatcher had said that this crew had been robbed a couple of times. Longarm stood near the engineer as the fireman stoked the boiler going out of Peacock. Longarm knew they were busy right now, so he kept quiet and just studied the passing scenery.

It didn't get interesting until they'd passed through the tunnel and rolled over the site of the last holdup. Longarm peered out the side in the bright morning light and, sure enough, there were more big boulders than a man could shake a stick at down in the dry creekbed to the right. The one they'd used to stop the train last night might or might not have some interesting scapes on her, if she was down there, and if a man wanted to spend the next few weeks poking at rocks.

As the track rose higher, they passed through a cut. The engineer said he'd been stopped here a week before. Longarm asked if they'd been headed out or coming down the grade. The engineer said, "Down, of course. They ain't hit us once on the uphill climb."

Longarm nodded. It made sense. Nobody was shipping horn silver *to* the mines.

"What about that tunnel back there? Anyone ever been stopped in there?" he asked.

The engineer said, "No. It's no mystery why. You'd be more likely to get a wreck than a stopped train if you put a boulder on the track in total darkness. Besides, if a train stopped in a tunnel there'd be so much smoke it'd be confusing as hell to both sides."

"Makes sense. You say they stopped you in that cut with a rock on the tracks, too?"

"Sure. That's the way they always do it. I ain't about to stop for no fool waving me down with a flag. If we could see the rascals in time, we'd just keep going."

"Yeah, a man would have a time boarding from a moving

mount on this dinky line cut out of the hillside. But tell me this: how come it's always such a surprise that the robbers are there, when you boys see that rock ahead on the tracks?"

"Hell, look at the slope above us. There's always rocks rolling down on the tracks. Nine times out of ten it's a natural accident. If you're asking why we don't plow on through, like that postal dick did, you don't know much about mountain railroading!"

"I can see why you'd stop for a big rock on the tracks," Longarm said, "when one considers the alternatives and how steep the off-slope is. You say that missing gent suggested you just keep going when you spy a waist-high boulder on the tracks ahead?"

"Yep. He said it was an experiment he wanted to try. Ain't that a bitch? It's no wonder the outlaws done him in. He was green as hell."

Crawford's notion struck Longarm as a mite reckless, too, but he put it aside to ponder later. He could see there might be method in the madness of not harming or robbing the passengers and crew after all. Nobody with a lick of sense was about to risk a serious fight, let alone an ass-over-teakettle roll down the mountain, if he didn't figure on getting hurt or robbed of his own. The cow catcher might or might not pitch a substantial boulder over the side without derailing the pilot wheels. It was a serious move to consider, even if one's life depended on it.

He asked the engineer if he had any notion what all the horn silver and dust the mines were losing added up to in dollars. The engineer said he had no idea, explaining, "It was took before it had been assayed or refined. So the figures could run a thousand or so either way. All in all, I'd say they'd robbed mayhaps ten to twenty thousand worth of horn silver and less'n five thousand in gold dust."

"Then no mines have been hurt more'n a thousand or so, right?"

"Wrong. Almost all the high grade comes from Triple Tits, up at the high end. They're working a particularly rich lode. The others along the line are in paydirt, but not hitting such pure stuff. A mining man I talked to says the grade peters lower grade as you works south. That's why they never found silver at all in the old Peacock mine south of town. The owners of Triple Tits have lost the most to the Timberliners, and they must be mad as hell about it."

"Are you fixing to pick up any high grade today, on this run?"

"Don't know. They never say till we get there. It ain't likely. You see, they don't dig the good stuff regular. They stumble over pockets in the regular ore as they muck. Then they set it aside till there's enough to be worth shipping, and...Yonder's Hanging Rock. Will you be getting off here, Longarm?"

Longarm said yes, as he meant to visit each mining camp in turn. So they slowed down. The engineer said they'd pick him up in a few hours on the way back. So, seeing that he didn't mean to stop, Longarm jumped off and lit running uphill toward the cluster of ramshackle buildings of Hanging Rock.

He could see right off why they called it Hanging Rock. The town was on the uphill side of the tracks, with a huge sheer cliff literally hanging above it, leaning out ominously above the little settlement. Longarm prayed it would stay like that for the next hour or so.

As he approached more closely he could see that he'd made a tactical error. There was less to Hanging Rock than he'd assumed. Unless the mine adit up the slope led to some serious digging, it wasn't going to take him any two hours to check out the property. A single ore car stood on a siding by the main line, half full, under a crude ore tipple. He traced the rickety trestle of the tipple up the slope to where its even narrower gauge entered the mine up yonder. As he was looking the ore car over, a Mexican packing a shotgun came up to ask him what in hell he thought he was doing. Longarm flashed his badge and said he was looking, and aimed to look some more. So the Mexican shrugged and lowered the muzzle of his scatter gun to lead Longarm up the slope.

They passed between about a dozen buildings. The most serious-looking one had a sign proclaiming it the general store and post office. The guard took Longarm to the entrance of the shack highest on the slope and knocked before entering. Inside, a fat man with the flushed face of a serious drinker lounged in a swivel chair with his feet up on a rolltop desk. As the Mexican wandered off somewhere, the fat man told Longarm he was the mine super and asked his pleasure.

Longarm said, "I mean to explore all the mines along the narrow-gauge. It's come to me that I started out the wrong way. I should have loaded my mount aboard a train, gone up to the end of the line, and drifted down the track with my own transportation."

"You mean even a famous lawman like you makes mistakes?"

"Hell, old son, everybody makes mistakes. Who told you I was famous?"

"Oh, word gets around. You'd be that Longarm who's come up here to catch them Timberliners, right?"

"Lord willing and the creeks don't rise. Do you mind showing me about?"

The fat man obviously did, but he got up with a sigh. "There ain't much to see," he said, "but let's get her over with. I don't know what you expect to find here in Hanging Rock. The Timberliners have never hit any of our shipments."

"You don't dig much high grade, then?"

"Hell, we're lucky to bust even. Come on, I'll show you the hole."

They went out and legged it the rest of the way up the slope. The super led Longarm into the mine. It was a simple straight drift following the grain of the natural strata in under the hanging cliffs above. They had two more Mexicans and a mule working it. The face was only a couple of hundred feet in and as they approached Longarm saw the miners were drilling. One held a star drill while the other hit it slow and lazy with a nine-pound sledge. It was easy to see why the ore car down the hill was half empty.

As if he'd read Longarm's thoughts, the super said, "This lode needs more modern methods afore it'll really pay."

Longarm nodded. "I heard it takes a gold mine to run a silver mine. How much are you taking out of this rock a day?"

"Hell, hardly enough to matter. I can't give you the exact figures. We just dig this infernal low grade and ship her to the smelters. They keep a tally on the tonnage. I doubt we're making a dollar on a ton, most days. Like I said, we're just about breaking even."

Longarm whistled softly and asked, "Why bother then?"

The fat man said, "Do I look like a cowboy? I need the job. That's why." He spat and added, "Might not have one, if and when they sell this hole. The owners in Denver have it on the auction block. My only hope is that nobody's fool enough to buy it."

Longarm bent to pick up a walnut-sized lump of ore. "Is this chloride?" he asked.

"I sure hope so," the fat super said. "It's the only kind of rock in the vein. Like I said, it's mighty low grade. To make this hole really pay, you'd need the manpower and machinery of a big operator. That's the only kind of outfit as would buy this claim out. The old bonanza days is fading fast. We've skimmed the cream of the Shining Mountains, and from here on, mining figures to be just another trade."

Longarm nodded in agreement. He knew big mining magnates were mining three percent ore and making it pay by buying the latest gear. But the future of the Hanging Rock mine wasn't his problem. He saw there were no side tunnels in here, so he asked the super, "Are there any old try holes in this neck of the woods?"

"Try holes? You mean them one-man shafts the prospectors dug in the young and foolish mining days? Ain't seen any around here. There was never what you'd call a rush in these parts."

"Do tell? How come there's mines all up and down the narrow-gauge if nobody prospected?"

"That's easy. When Lucky Larson tripped over an out-crop of horn silver up by Triple Tits a few years back, they naturally run rails up from the dying Peacock copper mine. Once the roadbed was cut, anyone with an eye for color could see how the same beds of chloride run from Triple Tits down to about here. The assholes who claimed this holding just about made her. The silver peters out to the south. It damn near peters out here and now."

"You mean each mine gets richer as you work north?"

"That's about the size of it. Of course, it ain't solid silver all the way to Triple Tits. The mountains got sort of churned up by something a spell back. So you can't just dig any old place."

Longarm had already figured that out. So he said he'd seen enough in the Hanging Rock mine and they went back outside. Longarm asked if the missing postal inspector, Crawford, had been up here having a similar conversation.

The super nodded and said, "Yep. About a week ago. Oh—I see what you mean about try holes."

"Yeah. If he was still alive, he'd have contacted his office by now. If he was dead out in the open, someone would have found him. They tell me in town they looked."

"Well, a posse did ride by here, and you can see how bare the slopes are all about."

Longarm stared downhill across the tracks, to where the land dropped off abruptly to the dry creekbed hundreds of feet down. He asked, "Has it rained up here in the last few days?"

The super shook his head. "They thought of that. It thunderstorms a lot up here and there was maybe a quarter of an inch of rain since that post office dick dropped out of sight. It was enough to cover any tracks he might have left, but not enough to fill the creekbeds. They looked for bodies down amongst the rocks. Didn't find none."

"Ain't there pockets among the boulders where a man-sized something could lodge in any kind of rain?"

"Sure there are. The boys up here know where they are, too. I know it's bleak up here, but we ain't in unexplored territory, Longarm. In mining country, folks poke about a lot. Give Marshal Bordon credit for some common sense. That missing gent ain't missing anywheres easy."

The super was staring wistfully at his office shack, so Longarm thanked him and let him get back to his desk and bottle. Alone and fancy-free, Longarm wandered down to the general store and post office, consulting his watch and cursing his own lack of foresight.

He went inside. The store shelves were half bare and a skinny dishwater blonde gal came out from the back looking hopeful. Longarm asked her if she sold tailor-made cigarettes.

She sighed and answered, "Surely you jest. The boys up here can barely afford cut plug."

Longarm said he'd take some cheroots to cheer her up, for she sure looked downhearted. "I noticed some of the dwellings about us are boarded up, ma'am. Could you tell me how many folks live here in Hanging Rock?"

"Not enough. Just about everyone's moved away and we'd be ghosted total if the mine closed all the way down." She thought and added, "I'd say there's maybe two dozen of us left now. You're right about most of the shacks being empty. Miners are funny. They leave when they don't get paid regular."

He put the extra cheroots away and said he'd take a box of .44-40 rounds while he was about it. As she handed them over, he paid, and then asked if she'd sold any other such ammo in recent memory. She shook her head. "No, but if the primers are dead, bring them shells back and I'll credit you for 'em. Is there anything else I can do for you?"

"Well, I don't have any letters to post. But tell me something. Does anyone have a key to the empty shacks, ma'am?"

"Sure. I do. They was left in my safekeeping. The mining company's trying to sell the property, and they asked me to make sure nobody salvages the quarters in the meantime. My name's Thelma, by the way."

"Howdy, Thelma. You can call me Custis. I'm a deputy

U. S. marshal and I got reasons for wanting a look-see in those boarded-up shacks."

Thelma nodded, reached under the counter for a ring of keys, and came out to join him. "I know what you're looking for. A post office inspector was up here a few days ago and I showed him around, too."

Longarm said, "I can't say what he was looking for, but I'm looking for him."

She blanched. "You mean he's dead in one of them shacks?"

"Could be. I'll go alone if you have delicate feelings."

Thelma shook her dishwater curls. "I'll go with you. It'll be a welcome change from staring at four walls, and I don't expect we'll find anyone dead in town. You may have noticed how small Hanging Rock is, and I've got a delicate nose, too."

She was right. They explored one empty shack after another, and all there was to see was dust and such furnishings as were too heavy to carry off in a miner's pack. The company had provided coal stoves, plank tables, and iron bedsteads. Most of the mattresses had been rolled up and taken away. The shacks were all built on the same two-room plan. They were on short stilts because of the slope, so it was easy to peer under the floorboards, and Crawford was nowhere to be found.

They got to the last shack. The only difference was the the family who'd moved out had left more behind. There were some prints on the walls and a bare mattress was still on the bedstead. Thelma sat down on the bed and said, "Well, that's all there is. What do you want to do now?"

Longarm consulted his watch. "Damn, that train won't be back for over an hour, and it's too far to walk back to Peacock. I don't suppose there's a handcar anywhere about?"

"Handcar? Not hardly. Why don't you set a spell by my side while you wait for the train, Custis? It ain't like you're pressed for time, right?"

He stared down at her thoughtfully. She met his gaze

with a roguish grin. From up here he could see down the front of her gingham dress better, and she was flat-chested. On the other hand, she was sort of pretty in a washed-out, tired way. He smiled. "I'd best remain standing, Thelma. Sitting next to a pretty gal has an unsettling effect on me. Uh—you didn't say if you were married or not."

She said, "I'm not. I used to be, but he got killed in a gunfight a year or so back. So I feels sort of unsettled, too."

"Oh? I can see you've been sort of lonesome up here, Thelma. I'm sorry to hear about your man getting gunned. What was the fight about?"

She met his gaze level. "Me. He caught me holding hands with somebody. I've ever been a warm-natured gal, and the man I married wasn't doing right by me. It got even worse after the fool got shot trying to bust up my romantic life. The law hung my lover for shooting him, and now I ain't got nobody."

She licked her lips, eyes glittering, and added, "At least I ain't till now."

"That's mighty forward, Thelma."

"I know. But you said you was fixing to catch a train in an hour. How many chances do you think I gets up here in this infernal ghost town?"

He didn't answer. Thelma started unbuttoning her dress as she pleaded, "Come on, honey, don't be bashful. I ain't *that* ugly!"

He laughed. "Hold on. I never said you was ugly, and I can think of worse ways by far to kill an hour. But let's lay out some ground rules here. I wouldn't want to get a lady's hopes up about the future, Thelma. I'd best say up front that I'm a wandering-on cuss, even when I ain't on duty, which I am."

She raised her thin rump from the bed to slip her skirts up over her head as she answered, her voice muffled momentarily. "I ain't asking for an engagement ring, damn it! *I'm* a love-'em-and-leave-'em cuss, too!"

Then, as she threw the dress aside to recline back naked on the dusty mattress, Thelma added, "Besides, I'm sure you'll manage to come back for a visit now and again, once you see what I has to offer."

She was built nicer in the flesh than her shabby dress had revealed. He knew she'd never forgive him if he didn't take his own duds off now, so he sat down beside her and did so, just to be polite.

It had all happened so fast that he hadn't really risen fully to the occasion by the time he hauled his pants off and dropped them over his gun rig at the head of the bed, for a pillow. He felt a mite shy and awkward, undressing in broad daylight in front of a naked stranger. But then Thelma was all over him, sobbing with desire, and they didn't feel like strangers any more.

Thelma wanted to get on top right off, so he let her. Staring up at her thin body with her almost scrawny thighs spread to receive him made a wild contrast to the soft Livia Bordon he'd had the night before in the dark. As she settled on his shaft, old Thelma closed her eyes, threw back her head, and gave a wild war whoop as she started riding him hard, tossing her blonde curls like a mustang mare in heat.

"For God's sake, not so loud! Someone might hear you!" he said.

She laughed and replied, "Who's listening? There's no-body about but us, and I'm about to screw you into the ground, honey!"

It was easy to see how two men had died fighting over her skinny body. Thelma had a hungry little love box that sucked like hell on the rise and slid down the firepole hot and kissy. He discharged his weapon quickly, considering how little time she'd given him to prime it. She yelled that she was coming, too, but she showed mercy to neither of them as she kept going, so Longarm lay back, bemused, to let her do all the work as he admired the view.

Thelma's sassy little breasts were too small and firm to bounce worth mention. But there was nothing boyish about her skinny frame. She was just a good twenty pounds lighter than the last gal he'd enjoyed, and she took full advantage of this to bounce faster than most girls could have.

He wondered if the missing Crawford had gotten any of this in passing. It hardly seemed likely he hadn't. Crawford had made all the other smart moves so far. Thelma had said she hadn't been getting any lately, but Longarm knew better. No gal screwed this well without regular practice.

She finally ran out of breath and rolled off, panting and begging for more. So Longarm rolled atop her to see if he could satisfy her. That turned out to be impossible. She was still carrying on crazy when he said, "I got to catch me a train, honey."

"Don't stop! I want more!"

"I noticed. I'd like some more, too," he lied, "but I'm on duty, and we'll have to finish another time."

As he rolled off and reached for his duds, she rubbed herself against him. "Do you promise you'll come back tonight?" she asked.

"I'll try, Thelma. But don't hold me to it. For one thing, I ain't a free agent. There's a gang of rascals out in the hills with guns. I could get lucky, or they could get lucky, Either way, I'm likely to be tied up with less pleasant business."

"Will you come back and see me some more when you can?"

He kissed her. "Well, I don't know how much more of you I could still see, but I'd be proud to try in another position. So why don't you think up one we ain't tried while I tend to my chores?"

That seemed to satisfy her enough to make her let go of him. So he got out to the tracks, still buttoning his vest, just in time. The train coming down the grade slowed enough for him to swing aboard. As he climbed up to the cab they told him they hadn't picked up anything much at Triple Tits, and they hadn't been held up, so far.

Chapter 9

Longarm glanced outside as the locomotive picked up speed on the downgrade. He frowned but held his tongue until they were going more than forty miles an hour. Then he nudged the engineer and said, "Slow down. You're going too fast for the roadbed."

The engineer frowned at him. "We always open up on the downgrade. Who's driving this locomotive, you or me?"

"Me," Longarm said. "I'm a U. S. peace officer and I'm paid to keep the peace. There's nothing peaceable about leaving the tracks on a mountain railroad, and you're rolling way too fast for a narrow-gauge track with flat and many curves."

"Shoot, Longarm, I've made this run a hundred times or more and I ain't never run off the tracks once."

Longarm reached past him firmly, and grabbed the throttle. "I ain't worried about you making it to the bottom of the grade or not, friend. There's other folk riding in the combination behind us, and they have a constitutional right to reach Peacock alive."

The engineer gasped, "God damn it! You can't commandeer my train like this!"

Longarm pushed him back farther and said, "Sure I can. I'm bigger and meaner than you."

The engineer turned to the fireman. "Are we gonna let this sassy lawman treat us like this, Mike?"

The fireman shrugged. "Leave me outten it. You just said yourself he's a lawman, and it *is* a nine percent grade."

They were still arguing, but Longarm had slowed down sensible by the time they rounded a blind bend and he spied something on the tracks ahead. He swore and hit the brakes as he threw the reverse lever, yelling, "Hit the deck, boys! I don't mean to step down peaceable!"

The Shay skidded to a halt just yards from the small but deadly gadget he'd spotted just in time. Longarm crouched in the doorway, gun drawn, as he braced for action from the rocks up the slope.

Nothing happened for a time. The engineer looked up from where he'd taken shelter in the tender gate and whispered, "How many of 'em are there this time, Longarm?"

"Can't say. I don't see a soul," Longarm said. "Mike, peer out the downhill side and tell me what you see."

The fireman did as he was asked, but reported, "Nobody between us and the creekbed down below."

The train conductor came up the trackside path, demanding to know why they'd stopped. Longarm called down, "There's a derailer on the track ahead. Since you ain't been shot, I'd say this ain't a holdup. Some son of a bitch was just out to spill us off the mountain."

The conductor, who was either brave or stupid, swore and moved down the tracks to bend and pick up the derailer. Longarm called, "Don't throw her away! Bring her back and I'll show it to the yard men, and they'd better have some good answers about their gear."

The conductor climbed up to join them and handed the device to Longarm. He tossed it aside without much study, since he'd seen derailers before. They were kept in most yards as emergency gear. When all else failed, you could stop a runaway car by clamping the viselike jaws of the derailer to one track so that the wheel flange hitting it was lifted and shunted off the track.

The conductor asked, "Who'd want to derail us and spill us down amongst them rocks? *That's* no way to rob a train!"

Longarm said, "I know. They weren't out to rob us today. That derailer was put in our path to murder everyone aboard this train." He released the brakes and opened the throttle again as he added, "We may as well be on our way. The would-be killer's long gone. I mean to stop at the edge of the yards to let the passengers get down, if it's all the same to you."

The conductor asked, "What for? Why are you at the controls, and how come you want my passengers to walk so far?"

"I always wanted to be an engineer when I growed up," the lawman said. "I'm stopping short because I want a good look at each and every passenger as he or she gets off."

"Jesus, do you suspicion someone aboard this combination is in league with the Timberliners?"

"Not hardly. It's what us lawmen call the process of elimination. I got way the hell too many suspects on this line as it is. Hopefully I might be able to whittle my list down a mite by discounting."

Mike, the fireman, said, "I get it, Longarm! Anybody aboard *can't* be riding with the Timberliners. The train robbers wouldn't want to kill one of their own bunch."

Longarm thought he'd just said that, so he didn't answer. After they were through the tunnel and within sight of town, he turned the controls back over to the engineer. He didn't want to get him fired and he wanted to hit the ground ahead of the other passengers. So, as they rolled into the yards, he said "Stop here," and jumped off.

He hit running and slid to a stop cursing, for the fool engineer didn't stop. He meant to pull into the open-shed station as usual, the mule-headed bastard!

Longarm started running. It wasn't far. He got to the platform as the other passengers were still getting down. Some were already legging it into town, so Longarm couldn't see their infernal faces. He recognized Al Wrenn from the hardware store. Wrenn spotted Longarm, too, and called out, ashen-faced, "What was going on back there, Longarm?"

Longarm swung wide of him, snapping "Tell you later!" as he headed for the locomotive up ahead. The engineer was getting down, looking smug. Longarm drew his .44, threw down on him, and said, "You're under arrest. Start marching toward the jailhouse, if you don't aim to be carried!"

The engineer laughed and sneered, "Shit, you can't arrest me!" Longarm pistol-whipped him across the face, sending him to the planks. Then he kicked him in the head as he tried to rise. The engineer went limp and just lay there, unconscious.

As people started to crowd around, one of Marshal Bordon's deputies, the one called Steve, elbowed through to ask what was going on. Longarm pointed down at the engineer, holstered his weapon, and said, "He wouldn't come quiet. I'd be obliged if you carried him over to your town lockup."

"Proud to, Longarm—but what's the charge?"

"Obstructing justice, federal. So I don't want to hear any bullshit about a local writ. When I tell a man to do something and he don't do it, he stands trial for it at the First Federal District Court of Colorado. Are you going to do as I say, Steve?"

"Hell, yes, I said I would. You sure are acting proddy today, Longarm."

"I know. I generally get proddy when somebody tries to kill me."

The fireman, Mike, cleared his throat. "I'm sure he was just funning you, Longarm. You don't suspicion of him of being in on the holdups, do you?"

Longarm said, "It don't matter one way or the other now. The son of a bitch is going to jail and the son of a bitch is staying there till I find out just who's with who in these parts."

Leaving the town law to tidy up after him, Longarm

strode toward the main street, trying not to smile. He knew the engineer was just a mule-headed show-off, but it was time folk started paying attention to his orders around here. He'd found in the army that the best way for a new top kick to shape up a sloppy outfit was to land with both feet on some sassy recruit so's the others could get the message that it wasn't wise to talk back any more.

As he headed for the Western Union offfice, another town deputy came running his way. Longarm thought he'd heard about the disturbance at the platform and was on his way to help. But the deputy, Dave, ran up to him and gasped, "Thank God you're back! It's awful! We don't know what to do!"

"About what, Dave? What happened?"

"Marshal Bordon! They just found him on the Tolland trail! Some son of a bitch just pumped him full of rifle balls, and he's deader than Confederate money!"

The undertaking parlor, if you wanted to call it that, was next door to Al Wrenn's hardware. The sign over the door read, T. S. SMILEY—GENERAL CONTRACTOR, PLUMBER, & FUNERAL DIRECTOR. Half the town seemed to be on the walk out front, but Deputy Pete and another Longarm didn't know were keeping them away from the entrance. Naturally, they let Longarm and Dave in.

Marshal Bordon was in the back workshop and sometime morgue with a lawman from Tolland and a man in a rubber apron who had to be the undertaker-plumber. Bordon's body had been stripped. Longarm could see that he had two bullet holes in his chest. One round had taken him low in the ribcage and he might have survived it, given mighty good medical care. But the other had hit him smack in the heart. So it came as no surprise when the sheriff's man from Tolland said he and one of the boys out front had found Bordon flat on his back on the trail south of town.

The Tolland man said his name was Dobbs and that the sheriff had sent him and a sidekick up to see if the new federal man in Peacock could use any help. Longarm asked where they'd stumbled over Bordon.

Dobbs said, "Just north of the old abandoned Peacock mine. His hoss had run off. But that's no mystery. It's out front. One of the townies grabbed it when it come trotting home alone."

A short, portly gent came in to join them just then and was introduced as Doc Forbes. He moved to stand over the body, frowning. "Have you started embalming him yet, Smiley?" he asked the undertaker.

The man in the rubber apron replied, "Nope. Figured you'd want to look him over first, Doc. That's why we sent for you."

Forbes nodded and said gruffly, "Damn right. I'm the coroner in these parts, and we got to do things right." He took out a thermometer and began to take the dead man's temperature. Longarm didn't ask why. He knew a dead body cooled one degree an hour. Rigor mortis hadn't set in yet, he could see. He was glad. He didn't mind looking at folks who were stiff, but it was sort of unsettling when they grinned up at you. That was why doctors with delicate manners pulled the sheet over your face when you cashed in your chips.

Longarm felt a mite guilty as he asked if anyone had fetched Livia yet. He figured he could still face her over the corpse of her husband, whom they'd betrayed the night before, but that wasn't likely to be pleasant, either. He had to face her sooner or later, since his horse and his possibles were up at the Bordon place.

The deputy, Dave, said, "We sent word to his family. The twins said they didn't want to come. They said their mother was out of town, but that they'd tell her when she got back from Lost Hat."

Longarm frowned. "I'm missing something. What in thunder is Livia Bordon doing up in Lost Hat, and how come the twins don't want to see their poor dead papa?"

"That's easy," Dave said. "Livia owns stock in the Lost Hat mine, left to her by her first husband. She goes up there regular to see how they're doing. Stays with her former in-laws. As to the twins not wanting to look at the dead man, it stands to reason. You can see the marshal ain't too pretty right now, and anyway, the twins wasn't his real kin. They was his stepdaughters. Livia had 'em by her first man, not Bordon."

"Do tell? I took 'em for one big happy family at breakfast."

"Oh, they got along all right, I reckon. In life, the marshal might have been a mite stricter than the twins fancied. He said they was too young to spark with the boys, and chased more'n one away. But he was never suspicioned by the neighbors of beating the kids or even mean-mouthing 'em. But from their attitude right now, I'd say they might have been a mite resentful."

"Hmm. If the wife is up in Lost Hat, she must have rode up on the same train with me this morning without me noticing. Can anybody alibi the gals?"

Dave stared aghast and protested, "That's an awful thing to say, Longarm! Them bitty twins couldn't have gunned their own stepfather!"

"How come? Did you see who killed him, Dave?"

"No, but I seen him ride out of town this morning alone. He said he had to check something out in Tolland. Didn't say what. He looked mighty worried and said he was in too much of a hurry to jaw about it. As to the twins, I seen them an hour later on their way to the schoolhouse."

"School is out for the summer, Dave."

"Yes and no. The twins attend half a day of summer school with Miss Simmons. They failed their examinations this spring and have to make it up if they mean to graduate next year. I know this 'cause I heard the marshal, there, complaining about them being not the brightest little gals he'd ever met."

Longarm made mental notes to check on the gals—all three of them—later. Doc Forbes hauled out his thermometer, held it to the light, and said, "Dead four hours, rough."

Longarm asked the Tolland lawmen when they'd come upon the corpse. They said they'd ridden out of Tolland after breakfast and had come upon Bordon less than two hours ago. Longarm estimated the riding time, and they didn't work as suspects. He didn't see why they'd have wanted to gun a fellow lawman anyway, and even if they'd had a reason, they'd have had no way of knowing that they'd meet him on the trail. Bordon had left Peacock long after they'd left Tolland.

Smiley asked Doc Forbes if he could embalm the body now. The doc had a look at the bullet holes and said, "May as well. There's no mystery as to the cause of death, and it's fixing to be a warm day."

Longarm asked, "Could you get the bullets for me, Doc?"

Forbes looked sort of unhappy, so Smiley said, "I'll do it. Can it wait till I drain the blood and pump him full of embalming fluid? Won't be so messy that way."

Longarm agreed, swallowed the green taste in his mouth, and went back outside. Al Wrenn was in the crowd of curious people out front. Longarm nodded at Wrenn and said, "You was on the southbound combination with me just now, Al. Can you point out any others, here, who might have ridden down the grade with us?"

Wrenn looked puzzled but proceeded to oblige. Most of the men he alibied were unknown to Longarm, but he'd remember their faces in the future. Wrenn said, "Cal Thayer, the assay man, ain't here now, but he was on the train. Is it important?"

"No. I can see why an assay man would visit mines up the line, and I didn't figure old Cal for a crook anyway. An assay man who handles other folks' valuables has easier ways to steal than holding up trains. An old-timer like him would know that, and his license dates back a ways."

"Jesus, you checked that out already, Longarm?"

"Before I ever met him. It's routine to check on the easy stuff."

The railroad dick, Tom Carrol, elbowed his way up to Longarm, looking upset, and demanded, "What have you got one of our engineers in jail for?"

"Mostly for acting smart," Longarm said. "Maybe as a

suspect. Don't it strike you odd that an engineer on a line as gets stopped regular likes to highball down a twisty, narrow-gauge, Tom?"

"He may be a fool, but he could hardly be in cahoots with the train robbers. Had you not stopped him in time he'd have gone off the same mountain with you, right?"

"Maybe. I'm still holding him for being smart with the law. I'd say I was doing you a favor, too. Crooked or not, that fool has no business at the throttle of a Shay."

"Look, help is hard to get up here in the high country, Longarm. I'll chide him about his manners, but you got to let him out. We need him to run the trains."

Longarm shook his head. "No, you don't. You've got other engineers. What you're really worried about is paying 'em overtime. So let's hope I don't have trouble with any of the others. The son of a bitch I arrested stays arrested till I cool down or clear him, whichever comes first. I know you think I'm taking a prank mighty serious, but the man messed up a serious investigation. If I knew for sure who might or might not have been aboard that train, I'd be able to thin down the list of suspects who could have gunned Marshal Bordon while I was up the line."

He took out a cheroot and lit it before he added, "By the way, I left that derailer aboard the Shay in my haste. Have you had a look at it?"

Carrol nodded. "Yes, the fireman turned it in at the roundhouse. It's not from our stock. It's not even factory-made. Our maintenance crew chief says it was cobbled up from scrap metal by someone who must have worked on a railroad at one time. It was mild steel, so it wouldn't have lasted long in regular service. It appears they made it special to wreck that particular train."

Longarm frowned thoughtfully. "That's interesting. Now all I have to figure is why the hell they wanted to wreck us at all. There was no attempt at robbery, so they weren't after the ore coming down the mountain this time. They must have been after someone who was aboard the train."

Carrol said, "That's no mystery. They were after you."

"Could be. They've been acting sort of surly about lawmen of late, and lots of folks knew I was aboard. Do you have the dispatches on that trip, Tom?"

"The dispatcher has, over to his shack in the yards. I have nothing to say about running the trains. I'm only paid to guard 'em."

"I'll ask later which mines might or might not have shipped this morn. While we're on the subject of guards, could you tell me the names of any of your railroad dicks who might have been riding in the combo behind me when we nearly went off the mountain?"

"Sure. I sent McGee and Taylor up the line this morning. Do you want to talk to 'em?"

"Not right now. They couldn't have seen anything up there that I didn't, and it don't seem likely either one tried to derail a train they were riding on. Just wanted the names to whittle off my list."

Carrol nodded. "When you check on me, you'll find I never left my office until a few minutes ago when I heard about all the trouble."

Longarm smiled thinly. "What makes you suspicion I suspicion you, old son?"

Carrol flushed and snapped, "Don't bullshit me, Longarm. I know you thought I let you down that time we worked together on another case."

Longarm shrugged. "I did. But, since you ask, I put it down to inexperience, not double-dealing."

"In other words you're saying I'm an asshole, not a crook?"

"I never call a man an asshole *or* a crook unless I knows for sure, Tom. Suppose we forget that old case and concentrate on this one. I got enough on my plate without you bucking me."

"Damn it, I ain't been bucking you. You ask me and my boys to do anything and we'll do it. I'll admit we haven't been able to stop the Timberliners. But I ain't seen any federal agents hereabouts doing wonders. Up to now, I makes it one lawman missing and three lawmen shot, along

110

with one innocent bystander down in Tolland."

"I'm still on my feet, Tom."

"Then why don't you go catch them Timberliners, instead of making ugly cracks at innocent folks just trying to do their infernal jobs?"

Longarm hadn't noticed he'd been mean-mouthing anyone all that much. But he said it was a sensible notion, and headed up the hill to get his mount and his rifle.

Chapter 10

Longarm was riding the Tolland trail alone, or thought he was, until he was out of town a ways and heard hoofbeats behind him. He reined in and turned in the saddle to see the Bordon twins, Susan and Sarah, coming down the trail riding their ponies sidesaddle. As they joined him, Sarah—or perhaps Susan—said, "We saw you leave the stable behind our house and ride off without even bidding us a polite howdy. That was mean, Custis."

Her sister said, "My balls are missing, too," so he knew she had to be Susan. "Don't look at me," Longarm said. "I ain't got your balls, Susan."

Susan looked at Sarah accusingly. "See?" she said.

Sarah protested, "I didn't even know you had your durned tinfoil in the tack room. What would any of us want with your fool balls?"

Longarm repressed a grimace. He knew they were young, but they had to be a mite subnormal as well, considering their stepfather had been gunned close at hand recently, and they were arguing about tinfoil.

"Well, gals, now that you know I don't have your tinfoil in my possession, suppose you ride on home," he said. "I'd like to play with you some more, but I'm on duty."

Sarah asked, "Whatcha doing?" "Riding down to the old

112

mine," Longarm replied. "And before you ask, you can't come. Go on home and wait for your ma. She'll likely need some comforting when she gets back from Lost Hat."

"You mean about our stepdaddy? She was sore at him for drinking so much. Besides, she won't be coming back from Aunt Tillie's for a day or more."

Her sister added, with an oddly precocious smile, "We'll have you all to ourselves at the house till she gets back."

"Go on home and we'll talk on it later, then. I have to be on my way," Longarm said.

He rode on. They followed. He didn't stop, but he asked, "Have you gals got wax in your ears? I don't want you tagging along, damn it!"

Sarah—or Susan—said, "Pooh! It's a free country, and school's out. I reckon we can ride anywhere we wants to."

Her sister said, "We wants to ride with you."

So that was what the three of them did. Longarm cursed under his breath, but it would take longer to arrest them and lock them up for their own safety than it would to suffer their sass in silence.

It was easy to see, when they came to it, where Marshal Bordon had been gunned. Longarm dismounted to scout for sign as one of the girls asked what he was doing. He didn't answer. They had to have *some* feelings for a poor old drunk who'd never beaten them.

Some ants were cleaning up the dried blood spots on the trail and the bootheel marks left by two men had to be the sheriff's men who'd found Bordon dead on the trail. He found no other sign. Or, if it was there, the trail was too pounded for him to read it. A well-traveled wagon trace had countless hoofmarks and wheel tracks to choose from. He found a spent .44-40 shell along the edge of the roadway. It was fresh and smelled as if it had been fired recently. He put it in his pocket. It didn't mean much. The murderer had been inconsiderate as hell about leaving clues.

He mounted up and rode on to the deserted mine. It wasn't far. The tipple, trackage, and such had been salvaged, as he'd been told, so the adit was just a hole in the ground, a few yards up the slope. Longarm dismounted and tethered Copper to a juniper stump before he headed in.

He noticed that the twins were following him. He saw that the abandoned shaft had been salvaged of timbers, too, so he told them, "Stay back, damn it. If this fool hole caves in, one of us ought to be able to ride back to town and tell folks about it."

He moved down the slight grade, noting by the wan light from the entrance that the ceiling was solid rock and looked as though it figured to stay off his head for now. He heard the grit of shoe leather and turned to see the infernal twins following him, holding hands. He swore softly, but saw that they were getting childish fun out of defying him, so he shrugged and went on, saying, "Watch your fool steps."

He fished in his pocket for a waterproof match, but it turned out that he ran out of shaft before he ran out of light. It was gloomy as hell now, but he could see that the shaft ahead had caved in. A wall of jagged rocks and damp clay blocked further progress into the mine. He peered down at the floor. The floor was clay, the consistency of modeling clay, and he could see at a glance that nobody had been this way since the last rain. From the look and feel of the almost-dry clay, he could tell that rainwater ran down the slight incline from the adit, pooled here, and smoothed things out as it evaporated in the thin mountain air.

So nobody was using this old shaft as a hideout or hiding place after all. Bordon had been headed somewhere else when he was gunned, and those rocks from the cave-in hadn't been moved recently enough to account for the missing Crawford. Longarm turned to go.

That was when he noticed both the twins kneeling on the floor, playing with the clay like much younger children making mud pies. That didn't bother him. He had them down as a mite slow. What bothered him was that both of them had their skirts up around their waists, and they were wearing nothing under them.

Susan—or Sarah—wriggled her naked rump against the cool, soft clay and purred, "Oh, that feels so good!"

114

As Longarm stared, aghast, he saw that the other one wasn't making a mud pie at all with the lump of clay she'd clawed together. She said, "Try this for real fun, Sarah," as she held out a big, surprisingly realistic clay cock."

Longarm said, "I wish you gals wouldn't do that."

But Sarah spread her teenaged thighs and leaned back, trying to shove the clay shaft into her exposed little pussy.

She said, "It's a free country, and I likes to have fun with my pussy. But, damnation, this clay thing's too soft."

Longarm gulped. While Sarah was trying to make love to a mud dick, her sister was getting down to business with her fingers, jerking her fool self off right in front of him.

He said, "That's enough, now, girls." But they paid him no mind and, despite himself, he was getting an erection. "Damn, a grown man could go to jail for what I'm thinking," he muttered. He stepped around them and headed for the entrance, to leave the sassy things to their own devices. It served their late stepfather right for keeping them home so much. They took after their horny mother, and there was just no way to keep a horny gal from acting horny if she aimed to.

But he couldn't just ride off and leave the twins here unsupervised, could he? There was a killer or more out there at large, and any man who came by, saw the twins' ponies, and investigated, was as likely as not to take advantage of the poor things.

He turned and said, "Come on, gals. Stop acting silly."

That was when he saw they were acting silly indeed. Susan and Sarah had stripped down naked and were fondling each other's bodies.

"Damn it, gals, that's a crime against nature!" he said. "Didn't your mama never tell you that was wrong?"

Longarm shook his head in wonder. He moved closer and pleaded, "Listen, you got to mend your ways. The law takes what you two are doing mighty serious. Are you paying me any mind at all?"

They stopped and sat up, side by side, to stare up at him, wide-eyed and innocent. Now that they had their clothes off they didn't look very innocent from the necks down. The nipples on their perky little breasts were turgid and rosy and one of them was still fingering herself as he said, "You can't carry on like lizzy-gals. It's a crime against nature."

"Is fucking agin the law, too?" one of them asked.

He laughed despite himself. "It's frowned on, but they don't put you in jail for it. I know this is odd advice to give two maidens fair, but if the altitude has you both so over-active I can only suggest you find yourselves some boy-friends. Uh—you do know how to take care of yourselves, don't you?"

The one who was masturbating smiled and said, "Sure. Ma taught us how to keep from getting in trouble before she let the old man join us in bed."

Longarm gasped. "Great balls of fire! Are you saying the whole household, Marshal Bordon and all—"

"Well, he didn't screw us when he'd been drinking."

"He shouldn't have been doing it at all! Listen, don't ever tell anyone about the free and easy morals up at your place. I know there's more such going on than the law ever hears about, but most folks sort of keeps it to themselves and—what the hell—the poor man's dead. So let's not bury him as a dirty old man, even if he was, to a right surprising degree."

The twin who'd been playing with herself lay back on the clay, legs spread, and whimpered, "Oh, damn, let's not just *talk* about such matters. I'm fixing to come, and I wants to be serviced right!"

Longarm sighed. "Oh, hell, enough is enough!" he said as he unbuttoned his shirt. The twin who was still sitting up said, "Hot damn, are you fixing to lay us both, Custis?"

"May as well. I wouldn't want anyone to feel left out, and I can see it's my duty to get you gals straightened out on the primrose path!"

He dropped his gunbelt and duds on the clay and began his lesson in adult sinning aboard the one who was apparently most in need of guidance. As he entered her he felt less guilty. For if there was one thing this young sass didn't have to worry about, it was her virginity. She was built like a tinier edition of Livia in every way. But from the skill he felt in her tight little love muscles, he knew she'd practiced with more than her fingers in the recent past.

He held his weight off her, in consideration of her youth, at first. But as she started bumping and grinding and hugging him closer he let himself go and just plain laid her. She told her sister that he was much nicer at this than their late stepfather. So Susan—or Sarah—leaped on his back to rub her groin up and down Longarm's spine as she giggled and said, "I'm next, I'm next! You've done it long enough to her!"

That sounded fair. Longarm outlasted the first twin, and when she came, rolled off to service her hot and sassy sister. This time they came together. By then the first one was begging for more as she beat on Longarm's bouncing bare rump with her fists. But now that he'd given in to temptation, it was coming to him how low-down some might feel he was acting, especially if the three of them got caught in the act.

"That's enough for now," he said. "We'll do it right at the house tonight, okay?"

The one he'd just come in said, "Goody. You can sleep in Ma's bed with us until she gets home."

He didn't answer. His semi-sated erection gave a little involuntary jerk as he considered the full possibilities of the mother and two daughters playing four in a bed. It sounded awesome. He wasn't sure he could do it. But he knew he'd likely try.

As the three of them got dressed, one of the twins demanded to know which one he liked best. He hugged them both against him and said, "That's the best part about making love to twins. One's as fine as the other. It's sort of like making love to the same gal, with additional opportunities thrown in."

"When we get back home, will you eat one of us while you screw the other?"

"I'll study on it. Right now I aim to just see you home

117

safe and sound—or safe, anyway. Needless to say, what just happened was a secret, right?"

"We won't tell on you, Custis. We don't want no other gals stealing you from us, now that we have a handsome stranger again."

He almost missed it. They were out of the adit and ready to mount up when he frowned and asked, "Handsome stranger *again?* You mean you kids and you—uh—free-thinking mama have played this game with other than your late stepfather?"

"Surely. That nice Mr. Crawford from the post office laid us both—and Ma, too, we suspicion. He stayed at our house when he first come to town. Didn't you know?"

They mounted up and rode back toward town as he digested what they'd told him. He'd been right about Crawford not missing many bets in Peacock before getting himself vanished. It wasn't fair to think ill of the poor weak-natured cuss, after following the same path to perdition. So, all right, what did it mean?

The missing post office dick had gone over the same ground and seen the same things, including who put out in Peacock and likely up at other camps. The fact that the bawdy gals had seduced Crawford as well as Longarm didn't mean they knew anything about his disappearance. Old Livia was a bawd who naturally extended hospitality to any willing guests, and her sexy daughters were too simple to be hiding anything. Could the late Marshal Bordon have been jealous? That hardly seemed likely. By now he'd have killed a mess of folk if he'd gone in for gunning everyone his wife and stepdaughters tempted. There was an outside chance Bordon had gunned the other federal agent. But since he was dead, too, Longarm put it on a back burner for now. He knew Crawford had left the Bordon house and gotten as far as Hanging Rock—and likely that blonde, Thelma. It sounded more like Crawford had been onto something more serious when they vanished him. If Longarm could uncover the same thing, without getting killed in the process, he'd be that much closer to the Timberliners.

He saw the twins home, put his mount with theirs in the stable, and got away from them with some kisses and a promise. He wasn't sure if he meant to keep it or not as he headed down to the telegraph office again, cursing and muttering under his breath, "Damn it, Billy Vail, why can't you ever send me on a case that turns out the way it's *supposed* to? This ain't no simple mail-robbing operation. It's a pure infernal can of worms. Someone up here is fibbing to me, and everyone else is acting crazy as hell!"

Chapter 11

At the telegraph office Longarm found a wire from Denver waiting for him. They said the killers of the unknown gent in Tolland had been figured out as a pair of hired guns and drifters knowed as Spud Smith and Lynx Brown. Nobody figured those were the names they'd been born with, but they'd left a trail of disorderly conduct from border to border in their past.

Lynx had worked some as a union-busting company bully and for a time as a private detective until losing his license for excessive zeal. Spud Smith had shot and beaten up fewer people, but was wanted for a killing in Texas. That was all for now on them. The man they'd gunned still lay unidentified in the Denver morgue. The office said they'd contacted some theatrical agents and, so far, hadn't found anyone who'd ever heard of a Gaylord Jones. Marshal Vail had added a personal warning to be on the lookout for Kandy McKane, another hired gun. He was said to be missing from his usual haunts in Dodge after confiding to a lady who sold information as well as her body that he had a big job lined up in the Colorado Rockies. Vail had only a general description of McKane to offer. He was said to be tall, dark, and mean as hell.

Longarm put the wire in his pocket and left, running the

name through his mental file of wanted posters. He couldn't connect the name McKane with anyone he'd seen recently. The description fit most anyone who wasn't short and blond or white-haired. He was sure he'd have remembered and odd name like Kandy if he'd heard it in the past.

He went down to the schoolhouse and knocked. Beth Simmons came to the door, her hair sort of mussed and wearing a paint and plaster-spattered smock over the longer skirts he spied underneath it. She told him to come in, but added, "You'll have to forgive my appearance. I wasn't expecting company,"

He said, "I ain't company. I'm the law. What's up? And, by the way, do you live here in the schoolhouse, ma'am?"

"Heavens, no. I board up the slope. Why do you ask?"

"I noticed you always seem to be here. Is that paint I smell?"

She led him toward the front of the classroom toward what looked like a forest sprouting indoors as she laughed and said, "I'm working on the scenery for our play next week. That's why I've been spending so much time here. How do you like it so far? That backdrop is supposed to be the woods of Scotland."

He stared thoughtfully at the canvas scenery she'd been working on and said, "I've never been to Scotland, ma'am, but those trees sure look real. What kind of a stump is that yonder? It don't look like pine and it don't look like hardwood."

She sighed. "I do the best I can. I'm not a botanist."

"You mean you made it out of plaster and such? Well, I never! Why'd you go to all that trouble, ma'am? There's more tree stumps than you can shake a stick at, down along timberline for the free taking."

She smiled sort of snootily and said, "I can see you've never been too interested in stage productions. We make our props of staff so they'll be light enough to move easily when we change the scenes."

"Staff, ma'am?"

"Burlap covered with plaster and painted," she explained,

121

stepping over to the apparent stump and picking it up with one hand. "See? Our scenery's almost finished. If only that annoying Gaylord Jones would get here! I don't know how on earth we're going to stage *Macbeth* without an actor to play Macbeth, do you?"

"No, ma'am. Don't look at me. I was in an opera one time, but I don't fancy a life upon the wicked stage."

She dimpled and said, "I hardly think your accent would suit the usurper king of Scotland. But you say you once appeared in an *opera?*"

"Yes, ma'am. Shooting, not singing. I chased a crook into an opera house out California ways and we had it out in the middle of Ida, that opera about Old Egypt."

She blinked and asked, "Ida? Don't you mean *Aida?*"

"Something like that. They closed the curtain once I shot the rascal in the middle of a big scene. But the gal as played the princess was a good sport about it, considering."

Beth Simmons laughed. "I'll bet she was. Am I wrong in assuming you're a bit of a ladies' man, Custis?"

"Depends on the lady entirely. What I really came to check on was the Bordon twins. They say they spent the morning here with you. True?"

She nodded and sighed. "They did, for what good it did them, poor dears. I don't see how I'm going to gradutate them next year. They're very sweet but, I'm afraid, not too bright."

"I noticed that, ma'am. You heard about their stepfather getting shot about the time your summer-school class was busting up?"

"Of course. But what's that got to do with...Oh, my God, you don't suspect *me* of anything, do you?"

"Not hardly. First time I ever saw you, someone was trying to shove a runaway train through yon wall at you."

She looked relieved. "Thank heavens. I know you people have to check up on everyone, but, really..."

"Do you have anything you don't want checked on, ma'am?"

She blanched. "Whatever gave you that idea?"

"You did, ma'am. When you paled as you asked if I was interested in your past. You want to save me some time by telling me what you may be hiding, Miss Beth? You know, of course, I'm only interested in federal offenses. So if you've run off from a husband or something like that . . ."

She flushed scarlet and said, "I've never been married. I'm not running away from anybody or anything, damn it!"

He nodded. "In that case, you have no call to be so flusterpated. I'm only here to catch some murdering train robbers and—no offense—you just don't fit the picture."

He ticked the brim of his hat and headed for the door. But Beth was obviously upset. She followed him, stopped him in the doorway, and put a hand on his sleeve to say, "The drama club will be meeting here later tonight. Would you like to drop by, Custis?"

"What for, ma'am? I told you I ain't a good actor."

"I doubt that very much. The meeting will be breaking up about nine. Maybe you'd like to escort me home after?"

He said he'd study on it and left, scowling, as he muttered, "Now what in thunder's going on, damn it?"

Longarm wasn't given to false modesty. Too many gals had said they'd admired him for him to think he was ugly. But Beth Simmons hadn't started batting her eyes like that till he'd brought up her past.

As a matter of fact, *she'd* been the one who'd brought it up, not him. The gal was hiding something. Something she was scared he'd find out. So he marched right up to the telegraph office and started sending wires to find out what it might be.

He ate lunch in a hole in the wall across from the depot. The waiter was a fat old Mexican man, so he didn't have to fight for his honor as he stuffed his gut. He was washing down his chili with coffee when Doc Forbes came in to join him. The doc put two misshapen lead slugs on the counter between them and said, "They said you was in here, Longarm. These are the rounds we found in Bordon. I just signed his death papers. The cause of his demise was gunshot at close range."

Longarm fingered one of the slugs. "I didn't think he'd been stabbed with no ice pick. As we figured, these slugs can't be traced to anyone in particular. But let's study on how they got in him. He was hit twice, from the front, in broad day."

"Sure. Meaning what, Longarm?"

"Meaning the killer was someone he knew and had no reason to suspect of deadly intent. Bordon drank and had other bad habits, but he was a lawman. He knew a gang of desperadoes was in the area. He was riding off to do something about it when he was gunned. Add it up."

Forbes nodded and said, "Right. The men who found him said there'd been no signs of a struggle, and Bordon's gun was in its holster when he died. He met someone he knew on the trail. As they was talking, the other one slapped leather, and that's all she wrote. He was dead before he knew he was in trouble. One round took him in the heart direct. The other hulled his liver. So he'd have likely died from that wound, too, in time. Do you reckon that's why there were two shots?"

Longarm shrugged. "Most gunslicks fire two or three into you before they stop and study on it. Have you ever heard of a gent called Kandy McKane, Doc?"

"Never. Who's he supposed to be?"

"Gunslick, said to be headed this way. He's about my height. Said to be dark. That might just mean he wears dark duds. Far as I know, he's a white man."

Forbes said, "I'll ask around. Strangers stand out in these parts."

"I know. The hell of it is, nobody I talk to has seen anyone lately they don't know at least to nod at." Longarm picked up his coffee cup.

"You still suspect the train robbers are local boys, playing two-face?"

"They surely don't seem to be camped out in the hills around. How far are we from the nearest cow outfit down in the trees, Doc?"

Forbes thought. "The nearest would be the Rocking Z.

About eight miles down the slopes to the east."

Longarm frowned and asked, "Rocking Z? Ain't that the outfit ramrodded by old Jim Page?"

"The name rings a bell. I think he's the foreman down there. Why do you ask? Do you know this Page gent?"

Longarm nodded. "Rode with him one time. He's a retired lawman. Got crippled up in a gunfight and went back to less exciting work."

Forbes said cautiously, "More than one old cowboy and more than one ex-lawman has turned owlhoot, you know."

"Yeah, I know. But old Jim Page won't work. Like I said, I used to ride with him. Saw him pass up more than one chance at easy money. If old Jim's turned bad, there's just no hope for the human race. He wouldn't have anyone on his payroll robbing trains on the side. As an ex-lawman, he'd notice. So the Timberliners ain't getting the horn silver out through the Rocking Z range. Who's working the higher range to the west?"

Forbes pursed his lips. "Hardly anybody. There's a young gent called Scotty Gunn camped out with a herd of sheep between the peaks up there. The men who investigated ahead of you have already talked to him. He says he's not seen anyone ride over the Divide in recent memory."

"I'd best ride up and have a word with him. Do you have a mount I could borrow, Doc? I don't want to go up to the Bordon house just yet."

Forbes, bless him, didn't question Longarm as they went out and over to the livery where Forbes loaned him a spare buckskin mare and a fair stock saddle. As Longarm led the buckskin out and mounted up, Forbes said, "Be careful when you talk to young Scotty, Longarm. The boy is a mite strange."

"What's the matter with him? Is he loco, or just feebleheaded?"

"Oh, you know how sheepherders are. He's never hurt anybody, but he is inclined to peg shots at folks he don't know personal."

Longarm thanked the doctor for the advice and rode out,

debating whether he should stop by the house after all for his Winchester. He decided he'd better not. The twins would only want to drag him to bed, and the air up here was making him feel crazy, too. He didn't have time to waste on such foolishness, even though he was feeling horny again after talking to that pretty schoolmarm.

As he rode up the steeper rise west of Peacock, he wondered what could be wrong with the young gent he was fixing to visit. Longarm didn't share the unthinking prejudice against sheep men some of his cow pals did. He'd met more than one decent sheepherder in his time. But Doc Forbes had said this one was sort of strange, and Longarm knew lots of sheepherders had that reputation. He didn't know if they got like that from screwing sheep or resisting temptation all alone on the high range with nothing much else to think about for months at a time.

He could see how it would vex a man's mind, either way. He'd never been marooned with a herd of sheep long enough to know how he'd handle the problem himself. He knew he wasn't going to get any answers about that from the young gent he was aiming to drop in on. He had more important questions to ask, and there were just some questions no man had a right to ask another. But, damn it, how was he ever to find out if it was true what they said about she-sheep or not?

Getting up to the Divide was no problem. After that, Longarm had to study some as he sat his mount, staring out all about for miles. Everything but the blue sky bowl was various shades of brownish-gray, sharp-edged in close and misted by distance further out. Then he spotted movement in a saddle pass below and as his eyes focused a whole herd of sheep and a summer camp materialized like magic. So he nodded and rode down toward it.

As he approached, a small black dog ran up the slope, barking, and a poncho-clad figure stepped out of the tent to call out, "Hold her right there, mister!"

Longarm reined in. The sheep dog ran around his mount at a safe distance, sassing horse and man with worried yips.

The sheepherder's voice was high-pitched and anxious. "State your name and business, damn it! Nobody invited you up here, and you're spooking my critters!"

Longarm saw that the sheep all about were just grazing quiet. He called back, "I ain't spooking shit, old son. Your hound and you are all that I see acting spooked. I'm Custis Long, deputy U. S. marshal. And I mean to jaw with you whether you like it or not. So call off that mutt, if you value it, and let's cut this bullshit."

Scotty Gunn whistled and the black dog ran off, looking innocent, to sniff at a lamb. Longarm rode in, dismounted, and shook hands with Scotty Gunn, who looked like a boy of maybe fourteen or so. It was no wonder the poor little cuss was nervous, being alone up here. He didn't look like he'd be much in a fight with a grown man, and there were all sorts of mean-hearted gents in the mountains, even when nobody was robbing trains in the neighborhood.

To assure the proddy youth, Longarm insisted on showing Scotty Gunn his credentials. Gunn seemed comforted to learn that he was a real lawman. He invited Longarm into the tent and poured him some surprisingly fine coffee as they sat on his cot together. Longarm took a deep gulp and said, "I needed that. The thin air up here makes a man's head feel queer."

"Are you saying I'm queer?" asked Scotty Gunn.

Longarm blinked in surprise. "Not hardly. What I rode up here about was the robberies further down. Anyone riding over the Divide would likely be noticed by you, wouldn't they?"

"They would in daylight," the young sheepherder said. "Crossing the Divide in the dark is possible, but it could ruin your health further down the slopes to the west. There's some nasty ravines and rock slides down below I wouldn't even want to try on foot at night, and I know this range better than any strangers could."

"I'm sure sorry you said that, son."

"Are you calling me a liar?"

"No. I'd say you just eliminated one escape route on me.

I'm running out of them. Someone's packing a mess of horn silver out of the vale below. But they can't go east, they can't go west, and someone surely would have noticed if they went north or south. That leaves us straight up. But that don't seem likely."

"I swear I'm not in cahoots with them, Long."

"Jesus, you sure are as proddy as they say, boy! Who in hell ever said they suspicioned you? I was told in town you're a regular feature up here. They said you was a nice young gent, sort of."

"Oh? What else did they tell you about me? Did they call me a queer?"

"No. Are you?"

"That's a hell of a thing to ask anyone."

"Don't keep bringing it up, then. I know some gents pick on sissies, but that ain't my style. So it don't matter to me one damned way or the other if you are one damned way or the other."

Young Scotty edged away and asked warily, "You ain't that way yourself, are you?"

Longarm snorted in disgust and was about to say he had better things to do than ride all the way up here to bugger boys. But he saw how upset the kid was, so he said gently, "You have my word I only screws women. I ain't even interested in your sheep."

He saw tears, real tears, in Scotty's eyes. "Jesus, you have been scared by somebody, haven't you?" he said more gently. "You want to tell me about it, son?"

Scotty Gunn did. The long, disjointed tale didn't surprise Longarm as much as it sort of bored him. Longarm knew young boys with girlish faces and mincy ways had a lot of trouble with degenerate drifters. Boys on a cow spread or even in jail could sometimes get an older, decent cuss to protect them. Young Scotty was all alone up here, and there were men who only had to hear about a boy alone and they got all sorts of queer notions. So far, Scotty Gunn had managed to be safe without having to shoot any unwelcome visitors. But it was easy to see why he was spooked about strangers dropping in without an invitation.

Longarm put down his tin cup, lit a smoke, and said, "Well, as I see her, you've either got to grin and bear it till you start shaving regular, or go into a less lonesome line of work."

Scotty sniffled. "I have to stay up here with the herd, damn it. They belong to my widowed mother down in Ward. My brother, Ian, is grazing the rest of our sheep up in Cameron Pass."

"Do tell? Seems to me you boys would have safety in numbers if you grazed your sheep consolidated."

"A lot you know about sheep. We're not allowed grazing licenses below timberline in Colorado, and up here amid the peaks the grass grows so spread-out that a sheep has to wander some bewixt bites."

"Yeah, I noticed the range was mostly granite scree. But you've answered one of my suggestions. You seem to be stuck with the job for now. How old are you, Scotty?"

"Twenty-three. Why?"

Longarm didn't answer. He'd lied about his own age when he'd joined the army that time. But this kid was ridiculous. He took a drag of smoke, shook his head wearily, and said, "Like I said, the thin air makes a man forget his manners. I forgot to offer you a cheroot, pard."

"That's all right. I don't smoke," Scotty said.

"Not even cigarettes?"

"No. I don't know how to roll a cigarette."

"Have you noticed anyone in these parts who does smoke them bitty things? Maybe one of the rascals who came up here to pester you? I have a reason for asking."

Scotty shook his head. Then he frowned and said, "Wait a minute. I did see some cigarette butts a spell back. I noticed 'cause there were so many of them. It was way down the slope as I was leading the herd up here about a month ago."

"Oh? What was this place somebody cluttered up with cigarette butts, Scotty?"

"Beside the trail, above Peacock. There's an old boulder

129

beside the trail and you can sit there and gaze out over the whole layout. As I come up, I remember wondering why someone had set there for what must have been a right long time. Just setting there smoking and not moving, you know?"

Longarm nodded and said, "One member of the gang smokes tailor-made cigarettes. I'd say you passed the rascal's last known address, Scotty. Now if I could just find somebody who could put him closer to us in time..."

"Do you reckon that gang will come up here, Long?"

"Hard to say. If they ain't so far, I don't see why they should."

"But they might. Oh, God, what will I do if they find me here alone?"

"Simmer down, boy. They're train robbers and murderers, not sissy-rapers. If it's any comfort, they've had more'n one real she-male gal at their mercy in recent robberies. They ain't trifled with the passengers. So I suspicion they ain't interested in such stuff."

A wind gust flapped the canvas of the tent and off to the west the thunderbird flapped its wings. Longarm sighed and said, "Shit!"

He wasn't surprised at anything the fickle summer sky above the high range might do, but his slicker was down at the Bordon house, lashed to his saddle. Young Scotty read the wind shift, too, and stood up, saying, "I have to bunch my sheep and hold 'em till that line squall passes over."

Longarm offered to help.

Scotty said, "Don't talk dumb. I'm wearing a poncho. You ain't. Stay in here and keep dry whilst me and Tinker hold the sheep on the mountain. It'll all blow over in a few minutes, but it'll be wet as hell whilst it lasts."

The young sheepherder had just ducked out when big, soggy frogs commenced leaping up and down on the canvas above Longarm's head. Then, having given fair warning, it commenced to rain fire and salt. The tent shook like it was aiming to pull up stakes and fly away like a bat out of hell. But Scotty had staked her too good. And when lightning sizzled so close that every hair on Longarm tingled, he was mighty glad the kid had camped in a saddle between two rises. A body could get struck anywhere up here when the thunderbird was flapping, but the odds were acceptable if the lightning had higher ground to spit at.

The storm lasted less than an hour, but that was still a tedious time to sit on a cot in a flappy tent alone. So, though he didn't have a search warrant and likely should have been ashamed of himself, Longarm poked about some in the sheepherder's possibles. He was looking for tailor-made cigarettes. A boy who lied about one thing could lie about anything, and if that unshaven face was twenty-three, Longarm was going blind. He didn't find any tobacco. But for a boy who was afraid of sissy-wolves, Scotty sure had sissy ways. Longarm wasn't above rubbing bay rum under his arms when he was expecting to meet a lady, but the bottle of violet perfume he found seemed mighty pretty. He found some well-thumbed little books with plain covers, too. They were dirty inside. Illustrated. It was small wonder the young rascal was strange-acting. He was up here all alone reading strange books.

The wind seemed to be dying, so Longarm put everything back where he'd found it. A few minutes later Scotty came back in, dripping. He took off the wool hat and poncho before he sat down, teeth chattering, and reached for some coffee.

Longarm said, "You're soaked from the knees down. You'd best take off them jeans, boy."

"I'd rather not. I told you I'm not that sort of feller."

"Damn it, neither am I, Scotty. What's the matter with you? Ain't you ever lived in a bunkhouse? Never mind, I can see you ain't. Go ahead and catch the ague if you're all that shy. When I get wet I take my duds off. I've done so in an army barracks full of men and nobody's ever buggered me yet."

Scotty blushed scarlet. "Please don't talk dirty. It makes me feel funny."

131

"All right. I'll be on my way as soon as it stops raining. I have another question. You say your brother's holding another herd of sheep to the north. Could he drive down this far to meet you without dropping below timberline?"

"Of course not. Sawtooth Mountain and some others are in the way."

"All right. How did you get down here from Ward?"

"Along the roads through the timber, of course. We're allowed to trail sheep through cattle country as long as we don't graze them serious down there. I followed the Jimtown trail as far south as the Rocking Z spread and then cut west. The cowhands on that particular spread poke fun at me, but they're not really mean."

"I know their ramrod, so I ain't surprised. You run your sheep up through Peacock along that same trail I used today?"

"Of course. What are you accusing me of, Long?"

"Not accusing you. Accusing them—the Timberliners. Tell me more about the trails to and from the north. If you had to, could you herd south from Ward and get into this country by way of Triple Tits at the north end of the narrow gauge?"

"Not hardly. The reason that camp's at the end of the line is 'cause there's a hell of a cliff just north of there. There's a mess of deep ravines, too."

Longarm nodded. Scotty's story matched with others he'd heard. The train robbers couldn't be using that route, either.

The wind had died down completely and the wet canvas walls hung limp about them in the suddenly stuffy tent. Longarm sniffed, frowned, and said, "Well, I'd best be going, ma'am."

Scotty gasped and flinched away. "Oh, how did you know?"

Longarm said, "Putting two and two together is my trade, Miss Scotty."

She looked down at the front of her loose, wet shirt. He

132

chuckled and got up from the cot to open the tent flap as he said, "Don't worry. Your secret is safe with me."

Scotty stammered, "I can explain why I dresses like a man."

But he said, "Don't bother. I can figure some things out for myself. Your ma is lucky her kids work so hard for her. The trouble you have with occasional sissy-wolves is nothing to what would happen should word get out a pretty young gal was playing Bo-Peep all alone up here."

He stepped outside and walked over to his tethered buckskin. The saddle was still wet, of course. Scotty had followed him out. So she saw what a wet crotched ride he was in for and suggested, "The leather will dry soon at this altitude. Can't you stay a spell?"

"Better not. Now that the cat's out of the bag I'd best confess I'm only human. You're a mighty handsome woman, Scotty. I'd best be on my way before my weak nature makes me say something silly."

She ducked her head and scuffed at the dirt with a boot tip as she said, "I thinks you're pretty, too. I don't reckon I'd mind if you could stay a while. Like you said, the damage is done."

He laughed, untethered the buckskin, then, seeing how forlorn she looked, he took her in his arms to kiss her adios. From the way she kissed back, he could tell he didn't have to leave if he didn't want to. But he turned her loose, mounted up, and rode off with a wave. Not because he was shy, but because it was time to act sensible—and, in truth, because she smelled pretty bad.

He told himself to forget about the sheepherder gal, for now. But the farther away he got, the less disgusting her smell seemed. But he kept riding. He wouldn't have been able to show so much strength of character had not he been so friendly with the Bordon twins that morning. But he had, and they'd be waiting for him in Peacock. Maybe even with their mother.

Wouldn't that be a bitch? He wasn't sure he could handle

all the opportunities the high country seemed to be offering him all at once. But that wasn't what he'd come up here to do, even if it was more fun than chasing train robbers.

Chapter 12

It was suppertime and the sun was setting when Longarm got back to the livery. As he gave the doctor's buckskin back he spied the rump of his chestnut police horse in another stall and asked the hostler what it was doing there. The hostler said Mrs. Bordon had brought it down from her place, along with Longarm's saddle and possibles, which were in the office. Longarm thought old Livia must be sore at him until the hostler added that she and her twins had locked up the house and caught the stage to Tolland. The Widow Bordon had come down from Triple Tits to say that she and her gals would be staying in Denver for a spell. They'd ordered Marshal Bordon's body shipped there, too, as soon as the next special ran down the narrow-gauge to the D&RG Western connection in a few days.

Longarm tipped the helpful cuss a dime and headed for the Western Union, cursing softly. *There's the trouble about trying to be virtuous, old son. Every time a man passes up on a temptation he lives to regret it. You could have had old Scotty there, but, you saved it all for your true loves, and now you'll be spending the night alone.*

He picked up some wires from Billy Vail, saw that nothing astonishing was going on down in Denver, and sent some messages of his own. Then he headed for the railroad's roundhouse. The streets were nigh deserted and the light was getting wistful and tricky under the ever-present overcast above the little mining town. It was the time of day when sober folk were going home. But he knew there was a night shift on the narrow-gauge.

He got to the roundhouse, looked into the offices at one end of the big half-moon facing the turntable, and saw that nobody was about. He wanted to talk to the dispatcher, so he went looking. He figured the dispatcher on the night shift might be checking things out before sitting down to his desk.

Longarm started with the roundhouse itself. There wasn't much to see. Two Shay locomotives sat under the tin roof of the semi-circular brick roundhouse. He knew the line had three. One must be out on a run. He eased between the tender of a Shay and the blank brick wall. He heard the grit of shoe leather on cinders, so he stopped between the two locomotives and turned. He started to call out, but he didn't. Whoever had followed him into the roundhouse was walking mighty sneaky for a railroad man on honest business.

Longarm drew his .44 as he stood still and listened. The unknown other had stopped, too. Longarm looked down, spied a coal clinker on the gritty cement, and bent to pick it up. Then he threw it over the locomotive behind him. It made a satisfactory clatter on the far side, like someone had tripped over something.

It worked. He heard more footsteps and flattened against the riveted steel side of the tender closest to whoever was tailing him. A million years went by. Then a shadowy figure appeared, gliding along the bricks with a Winchester at port arms. Longarm said, "Howdy, you dumb prick."

The tall man with the saddle gun gasped and tried to swing its muzzle before Longarm could fire. He didn't make it. Longarm's first round slammed him back against the roundhouse wall. But there was enough life left in him to slide sideways, back the way he'd come. Longarm followed, firing at will into the slot between tender and wall. It was hard to see in the smoke and gloom just what he was doing, but he must have been doing something right, for he heard the Winchester clatter on cement, followed by a dull thud. Then Longarm's hammer clicked on an empty chamber.

He ran toward the front of the locomotive instead of risking the smoke-filled slot. He didn't have time to reload. So he put the hot .44 in its holster and took out his vest-pocket derringer as he swung around the cow catcher. That turned out to be a good notion. For as he moved down the far side of the Shay he saw that the rascal he'd put on the cement was still alive and covering the smoke-filled slot with his own back-up. Before it could occur to him that there was more than one way around a locomotive, Longarm shot him in the ear.

Longarm knew he wasn't going to make any further hostile moves in the foreseeable future, so he started re-loading his weapons as he moseyed over to see who the hell he'd just shot. He rolled the body over with a boot tip and stared soberly down. The dead man had a couple of days' worth of beard and the one eyeball hanging by its stalk didn't do much for his looks, either. Longarm struck a match. The messed-up face looked vaguely familiar, but he couldn't match it up with any wanted posters he'd seen recently.

He heard running footsteps. That didn't surprise him. Fire bells and gunshots had that effect on some folks. "What's going on? Is anybody in there?" a voice called out.

Longarm recognized Tom Carrol's voice. He said, "In here. Watch where you step."

The railroad dick and the night dispatcher eased through to join him. Tom Carrol stared down at the corpse. "Jesus, who's that?" he gasped.

"I'm still working on it. He was after me with that Winchester against the wall. It's a .44-40, too. Did you boys come down the slope together just now?"

"Yes. Why?" said Carrol.

"Just asking. I don't suppose you know this gent at my feet, do you?"

Carrol bent to look closer. "Don't know his name, but

137

I've seen him somewhere before."

The yard dispatcher said, "Me too. I'm sure I've seen him in passing up along the main street. But he don't work for us or for any of the mines. What was he doing in my roundhouse?"

"Looking to gun me. He must have spotted me headed this way and figured it was a good time to get me alone. The reason I came down here was to look for you. I've got a dispatching favor to ask you."

What sort of favor, Longarm?"

"You know that once-a-week special you send down to hook up with the D&RG Western? Well, I want you to send her tonight. Can you do so?"

"What for? We generally wait for enough bullion from the smelter mills to matter before we use that spur, Longarm. That's why we only runs her now and again. It takes a dozen loads of ore down from the mines to the north to make a load of refined metal."

"I know that. I want you to do it anyway. Besides, Marshal Bordon's body is due in Denver and embalming fluid can only do so much in high summer."

"Oh, all right. I can use that as an excuse, I reckon. I have to account to the owners in Denver for my dispatching up here. But I'm sure they won't mind, given such a delicate reason."

The railroad dick said, "I have one objection, Longarm. You know I'm paid to keep things secure at this end. I can guard the bullion extra as far as the D&RG Western at Tolland. But what about all that bullion being sent down to the Denver Silver Exchange unexpected?"

"That's easy," Longarm said. "There's security men on the main line, and I'll wire the office to expect the bullion and see it gets safely to its owners. It might even surprise some folks who expected the shipment later in the week."

The dispatcher brightened. "Hot damn! I get it! You suspects an insider working with the Timberliners, so shipping silver unexpected might force his hand, right?"

"That's one reason. How soon can you get cracking?"

"I'll have to tell 'em at the mill so's they can load any recent ingots. What about this rascal on the floor? You want to send him down to Denver, too?"

"Might as well. I can give the local coroner an educated guess as to the cause of death, and I doubt anyone up here will come forward to claim the body. I'll ask some of the town law to come down and clean up after me. It's been nice talking to you boys, but I got a lot of bases to cover, so I'd best be on my way."

He went back to the Western Union office and brought his boss in Denver up to date. Then he went to Al Wrenn's hardware store. Wrenn was just locking up for the evening, and Longarm told him what had happened. Wrenn said, "You sure leads an interesting life, Longarm. What can I do for you? Do you want some supplies, or do you aim to send a letter?"

"Neither. But your post office sideline is what I came to see you about. I hear a stage just left for Tolland. Do you ship mail down there by stage, Al?"

Wrenn shook his head. "Nope. The stage don't run often enough."

"I noticed. But the special trains down the spur to Tolland run even less often. So how does mail get in and out of here?"

"Easy. I have a kid working for me part time who packs it once a day by saddlebag. If there's anything more important to write home about, most folks use the Western Union. Do you want to talk to my mail packer? I can fetch him for you if you do."

Longarm shook his head. "Not for now. He'd have likely come forward if he'd seen anything worth talking about on the trail. But, as long as I'm whittling, where was he when Bordon got shot?"

"Working here at the store. When he ain't packing mail I have him stacking boxes. He wasn't riding the trail the day the other gents got shot, neither. I know us civilians ain't supposed to play detective, but it's natural to talk about such things amongst ourselves. So I can tell you that nobody

I can think of was on the Tolland trail at the times you're worried about."

"Hell, Al, I ain't worried. Just whittling, like I said."

They shook hands and parted friendly, Wrenn to go home and Longarm to the assay office and mills. He'd been too polite to tell Al Wrenn the local vigilance committee was full of shit. Nobody in a town even this size could say for sure who might or might not have been accounted for at any given time. When you added up all the other folk living all along the line in other camps, it got worse. He had more possible suspects than he could shake a stick at if he stayed up here a month or more.

He'd told his boss true when he'd said he didn't want any assisting deputies. He still didn't. There were advantages to working alone. But he was spread out thinner than he'd expected on this case. There were too many places and too many folks to cover. He'd been bouncing all over like a ball and he still hadn't even visited half the infernal stops up the line.

He found old Calvin Thayer still open for assay business. But before he could go in, Tom Carrol caught up with him to say, "We found a packing crate to fit that rascal you just shot. He had no I.D. Just small change and a mess of ammo in the pockets of that dirty black suit. I assume you want him delivered to the Denver morgue?"

"You assume right. They have the facilities to keep him preserved till we can figure out who the hell he might have been. He matches the make of that Kandy McKane, but I'm holding off on saying it's him for sure."

"How come, Longarm? They said Kandy McKane was a killer headed this way to do a job, and he sure tried to do a job on you."

"Yep. That part fits. But I'm sure I've seen the son of a bitch in the past, somewheres. I never heard of Kandy McKane till recently."

"Try her this way. You saw him around Dodge one time and didn't know his name."

Longarm nodded with a frown and said, "Yeah, that works. Six or eight years back I was a regular visitor to Dodge, and they say Kandy McKane made his brag there. But forget about him. Denver will find out who he was."

"Right. Listen, about that special train you want sent south tonight. You've still got one of our engineers in the town lockup and I was wondering..."

"Oh, all right, tell the boys to let him out. But I'm holding you accountable if he messes up again."

"I doubt he will, now that he sees how serious you take it."

They shook on it and Longarm went into the assay office. Old Thayer was in the back, fooling with his test tubes. He smiled up at Longarm.

"Howdy. Be with you in a minute. Just finishing up a report on some produce from Hanging Rock."

Longarm found himself a seat on a stool and lit a smoke as the old man puttered on. Longarm asked casually, "Are they still getting color at all at the Hanging Rock mine? I was just up there and they looked sort of discouraged."

"They have every right to be," the assayer said. "It's a mighty low grade operation. But I have news that might cheer them some."

"Silver's getting richer under Hanging Rock?"

"No. There's hardly enough silver to be worth the drilling, using the old-fashioned methods. But I've assaying their refined ingots, and there's an interesting impurity."

"Do tell? What's mixed with the silver? Tin?"

"Don't be silly. There ain't no tin in the Rockies. What I've found is *gold*. Not a hell of a lot of it. Maybe one-half of one percent. But it's there. And the price of gold is up."

"I've heard that. So the half-dead mine is saved?"

"Well, yes and no. Like I said, it's still piss-poor rock. Some big outfit using the latest extraction methods and digging serious could turn a profit up to Hanging Rock. They don't figure to do it with the half-ass crew and tools they're still using."

Longarm blew a smoke ring, studied it, and asked, "Has any big silver syndicate been trying to buy any of the small mines up here?"

Thayer shook his head. "Not as I know of. The Denver stockholders in Hanging Rock have been trying to float a bank loan to buy better gear. So far, they've been turned down. Banks never lend money to folks as really need it. But this richer ore they've drilled into may tip the balance. That's why they'll be glad to hear about it."

Longarm searched for a delicate way of putting it, saw there wasn't any, and asked flat-out, "What are the chances the hungry owners have slated their own mine, Cal?"

Thayer looked more smug than shocked as he replied. "This may come as a surprise to you, Longarm, but I'm paid to think of things like that. In the first place, I was just up to Hanging Rock. I went as soon as their ingots started showing unusual color. Frankly, I don't think the poor hands working said mine have the brains to salt their ore. But, since anything is possible, I poked around. I stole some ore samples fresh from a blast."

He held up a test tube full of dark liquid, as if he expected it to mean something to Longarm. "There's the barest trace of gold in this ore sample. There ain't a penny's worth of gold and silver together, but it averages out the same as the ingots."

"Meaning what, Cal? I ain't a mining man."

Thayer put the test tube back in its rack as he explained. "When you salt a mine, you do so by coating the surface of the ore some way. I took the liberty of peeling the skin off the ore sample with acid before I crushed it and tested it for its metal contents. It's real. Low grade as hell, like I said, but worth digging. Some of the same ore came down on the train with me and just went through the mill. The resulting ingots assay in the same proportions. What made you suspect that particular mine, anyway? It's not the only one up the line, you know."

"I'm suspecting 'em one at a time."

Thayer nodded and said, "In poking through my papers

this morning I came across something I didn't know I had."

He reached into a drawer, took out a folded paper, and handed it to Longarm. "It ain't complete. I don't know what happened to the other sheets. But this one gives an overall picture of the old copper mine you've been asking everyone about."

Longarm unfolded the print and studied it for a time without speaking. The paper was water-stained and grimed. The brownish lines were hard to make out in spots, but it seemed to be a rough layout used to lay tracks and air hoses. There was no indication of ore bodies. But if they hadn't dug all the copper by the time they'd shut down, they never would have shut down. So what the hell. Longarm didn't see anything exciting. He folded the chart and put it away, saying, "I'll study it some more later. I had the impression you never worked for the copper outfit, Cal."

"I never did. That's why I was sort of surprised to find that in my old files whilst looking for something else. This office had been used before I moved in. The way I figure, someone from the copper outfit must have left it behind and it just got shoved out of the way as I was setting up."

"Well, sometimes I get lucky, Cal. You may have saved me a day or so of waiting."

"I hope so. But what were you expecting to see on that old chart, son? I looked it over careful, and I'll be damned if I see what good it can do you to know where the tunnels of a caved-in mine once ran."

Since Thayer had been so polite, Longarm took the time to answer. "I once worked another case involving abandoned mine drifts. A tunnel everyone thought was filled in wasn't. It ran smack under the only bank vault in town."

Thayer whistled. "That can be expensive! I see what you were after now. But, as you see, the Peacock mine never drilled anywhere close to town. Them drifts run mostly east and west, deep under the Divide."

* "I noticed. Is there any chance they might not have had every last drift charted? If you kept drilling long enough, you'd come out on the other side of the Divide, right?"

Thayer looked incredulous. "Don't talk foolish, son. I like you. Do you have any notion how deep a tunnel you're talking about? The Peacock would have been famous as hell by the time they'd drilled clean through the Continental Divide through thirty miles or so of solid rock!"

"I was up top this afternoon and I noticed distances tend to get out of hand up here. A spoil bank left by digging that far would be mighty noticeable, too."

"Noticeable? It'd be a landmark, like the Pyramids of Egypt. Aside from being caved in, the Peacock mine can't extend more than six or eight miles in any direction, and the chart says all the drifts dead-ended deep in the mountain."

Longarm thanked the assayer and left. He consulted his watch and went to have supper, feeling a mite wistful when he studied on the home cooking and other pleasures he wouldn't be getting at the Bordon house any more.

He considered just where he would quarter for the night and almost asked the waiter if he knew of a rooming house in town before he grinned to himself. The answer was so simple that he doubted anyone still gunning for him would think of it either. The Bordon house was empty and locked up. The tack room would be locked up, too. But he could get in by way of that loose board and spread his bedroll in the same corner.

That still left him sleeping alone—but, what the hell, it would make for a change. He finished his grub, circled the block to make sure he wasn't being followed, and headed for the schoolhouse.

He'd timed it just right. The Peacock Drama Club was still going at it fire and tongs as he came in and sat down at one of the school desks, doubling his legs some. He noticed the full cast wasn't present, just Beth Simmons and three other gals. They were practicing to be witches, as Beth directed. They looked silly as hell, crouched around a big papier mâché pot, cackling and cursing in Shakespeare. One had a right nice ass. But, from the way they were carrying on, Longarm was glad he'd turned down the chance to play Macbeth. Apparently the bad king of Scotland was supposed to be there listening to them tell his fortune, which was awful.

Naturally, without the missing Gaylord Jones, they had to carry on without Macbeth. Having nobody to swordfight with, Al Wrenn and the sissy young gent playing Malcolm hadn't bothered to show up. Longarm didn't care.

Beth Simmons had seen him come in, of course. After she'd let her witches cackle a mite more, she called out, "That's enough for tonight, ladies. There's really nothing more we can do to polish that scene until Mr. Jones arrives."

She introduced them to Longarm and served coffee all around. He was polite, but even the one with the nice ass was sort of plain, even acting human, so he didn't try to remember their names.

After a time they left. As the schoolmarm ushered them out, Longarm moved on stage—if you could call it that— and hefted the big pot with one hand.

Beth shut the door and rejoined him, saying, "Be careful, it's fragile."

"I noticed. Sure looks real, though. Who made it?" he asked.

"I did. Why?"

"Just being nosy. You sure have lots of skills, Miss Beth. You run a school, make scenery, put on plays named after yourself, and all."

"What are you talking about? The play's name is *Macbeth*."

"I know. And you're *Miss* Beth."

She frowned. "Heavens, I never even noticed Macbeth's name sounds something *like mine!*"

"You were thinking unconscious, I reckon. I catch folks doing it all the time in my line of work. It pays a lawman to have a good memory when folks fib to him."

Beth Simmons sat on the edge of a desk, staring down, and heaved a deep sigh. "All right, so you know."

Longarm didn't say anything. He had no idea at all what he was supposed to know. But another trick he'd learned in questioning suspects was to keep his damned trap shut when he didn't have a sensible question to ask.

Beth's voice was small and scared. "What happens to me now? I know you can't arrest me, but do you really have to turn me in?"

He sat down on the edge of another desk across from her and answered soberly, "I ain't sure. I don't think what you done was a violation of federal law. But suppose you tell me why you done it, Beth?"

She sighed. "I needed the job, of course. I know the school board said needed someone with the proper background, but I'd been looking for a job so long, and when I saw the ad in the paper..."

Longarm managed not to burst out laughing as he suddenly got the picture. "That's why you've been putting in all this extra work, then? To keep anyone from suspicioning you wasn't a real teacher?"

"Of course. Do you think I *enjoy* trying to make actors out of these poor yokels?"

"I can see you're better educated than most in these parts, Beth. Is Beth your real name, or did you make it up 'cause you'd acted in *Macbeth* so many times?"

She stared up at him and gasped, "My God, you're good! How did you know I was a stranded actress? You couldn't have checked on *that* by wire!"

"Didn't have to. I added it all up in my head. You talk and move like a gal who's had drama lessons. I've met small-town schoolmarms, too. They don't generally suggest Shakespeare plays if they put on any plays at all. Even the better educated ones hardly ever know how to make stage scenery, either. So let me put your tale together, for practice. You come out West with a touring road company. You found folks out here don't admire Shakespeare as much as they do *Uncle Tom's Cabin*. So you wound up stranded and broke. You already told me about snatching at the only decent job you could find."

146

She nodded. "My real name's Marie Marlow. What happens now?"

"Howdy, Miss Marie. I don't see as anything has to happen, as far as the federal government's concerned. It ain't like you've been teaching *Indians* under false pretences. But while I have you in a confiding mood, answer me some other questions. Is this Gaylord Jones of yours a real actor, or did you make him up, too?"

"He's my lover—or was, if you must know."

"That's not what I asked. Anyone can kiss a pretty gal. Is he really an actor?"

She laughed bitterly. "A better actor than I thought, it seems. I was sure he'd leap at the chance to join me up here, if only for a while. But, as you see, he must have other things to do, and— Oh, what am I to do on opening night, Custis?"

"Cancel it," he suggested. "You've been padding your part, like you acting gals say. I won't turn you in, and the folks up here won't suspicion you if you call the fool play off. You've got a good excuse and, by now, you must know folks out here ain't all that wild about *Macbeth* in any case."

She started to object. Then suddenly she threw her head back and shouted, "Wheeee! My God that feels good! I'm going to cancel the damned play! I have been padding my part, and you're right that nobody will care!"

"There you go. Let's talk about Gaylord some more."

She frowned. "Do we have to? I feel I can talk to you, Custis. You're a man of the world, despite your rough edges. I guess you know I only wanted to put on the play so I'd have an excuse to get Gaylord back. Now that it didn't work, well..."

He nodded, but she'd sent one over his head. "What do you mean get him *back*, Marie? I didn't know you'd lost him."

She shrugged. "I wasn't sure I had, until now. We broke up as lovers just before our tour ended in Denver. Some of the company had the money to get back East. I didn't. The last I heard of Gaylord he was working as a barkeep in

147

Denver. So, all right, call me foolish; I thought if I wired him that there was a part in a play, with free room and board thrown in . . ."

Longarm stopped her with a wave of his hand. He'd heard many a gal's version of this yarn. He studied on whether it would cheer her or not to learn that he suspected her Gaylord Jones had taken her up on her offer, and then been gunned by mistake in Tolland. He decided to hold off until he was sure.

He knew he'd made the right move when she suddenly said, "It's just as well he didn't come, I suppose. He really was no good for me. I knew I was being soft-headed when I sent for him."

"Why'd you do it, then?"

She heaved a defeated sigh, hesitated, then said, "If you must know, I was getting hard up. Haven't you ever been stuck in a strange town, alone, and started thinking of someone who, while maybe no damned good, was awfully *pretty?*"

He chuckled. "Many, many a time. I'm glad you weren't really in love with him. But what busted you up?"

"Chemistry, I suppose. You see, Gaylord is handsome, but sort of—ah—easy to satisfy. I think I may have made too many demands on him." She blushed. "My God, how do you *do* that? First you get me to confess I'm a fake teacher, and now I'm talking about my sex life. You must have hidden powers my poor witches could use lessons in. I don't even know you, yet I'm telling you things I'd blush to say to another girl!"

He rose, pulled her to her feet against him, and bent to kiss her full on the lips. She liked it enough to kiss him back with considerable skill at first. Then she drew away and gasped, "What do you think you're doing, you brute?"

He smiled down at her. "What do you want me to do? I ain't a brute. Like I told you before, it depends on the lady I'm with."

"Oh, are you saying I'm a hard-up, easy lay?"

"Nope. You said it. If I'm wrong, I'll turn you loose and we'll say no more about it."

She laughed, sort of wild, then hugged him closer. "Oh, hell, what's the use? I can see a girl can keep no secrets from you! But where can we go? I'll be damned if I'll make love in a schoolroom on a desk!"

It sounded like fun to Longarm. But in the end they got his bedroll from the livery, with her standing discreetly in the dark outside, and he took her up to the deserted Bordon house. She laughed when he showed her the secret way into the tack room. She asked how he'd ever discovered it and he said, "Mischievous girls showed me. We could likely get into the house, but somehow it don't seem right."

She slipped off her smock. "Hurry, darling," she whispered.

He spread the roll out on the floor in the corner and by the time he had Beth—Marie—whatever—had shucked her dress and dropped to her knees beside him in her underduds, which were a lot of fun to kiss her out of as she helped him shed his own things.

At the last minute, being a woman, she suddenly said, "Wait. I'm not sure." But he was used to such she-male notions, so he just kissed her good to shut her up till he was mounted right between her trembling thighs with their naked torsos pressed together as tight as they had their lips. Tightness seemed to go with the pretty actress gal. As she felt him entering her she rolled her head to one side and gasped, "Oh, no! I was afraid you'd be too big for me!" But when he stopped three-quarters of the way home, Marie braced her heels on the floor and thrust her pelvis up hard to take it all. As they started going at it right, he was glad he'd passed on that fool sheepherder.

For this one had told him true about being sort of demanding. She came fast, sobbed how glad she was that Gaylord had betrayed her, and proceeded to screw him silly.

He didn't mind as much as Gaylord might have. He'd been looking forward to some serious riding with two or

149

maybe three gals tonight. He liked being screwed silly. So it worked out right for both of them.

She said she'd never met such a tireless stud before, and, though he didn't say it, he had to admit that she was wild enough to do the sexual chores of both the bawdy Bordon twins, and likely even their mama as well.

Before she even stopped for the first smoke and pillow conversation, the gal had demanded every position that didn't hurt. The light was too poor to see her all that well, but it didn't matter. She felt kissy everywhere he could get his lips, and any gal who moved so fine would have been worth taking to bed had she looked like one of old Macbeth's three witches.

She finally showed mercy, after midnight, and he took her home to save her reputation. She made him promise they'd meet again tomorrow night. By the time he got to sleep he never wanted to see another woman as long as he lived. But he figured he likely would.

Chapter 13

Next morning, Longarm rode up the narrow-gauge alone on Copper. He felt a mite saddle-sore for such a long, tedious ride. But in the first place he couldn't see much in the time the railroad schedule gave him, and in the second, the Timberliners had never robbed a train going up the grade yet. He figured he'd ride to the end of the line on Copper, then load the horse aboard a southbound combination and get the best of both worlds.

The fact that the Timberliners might not be laying for a northbound train did not mean they couldn't be laying for him, of course. Longarm rode with his eyes peeled and his saddle gun across his lap, loaded and cocked. He rode through the tunnel just north of town, striking matches and taking more time. He didn't see anything interesting, and nobody shot him on the far side, so he kept going.

He got to Hanging Rock, but he didn't stop. He'd looked at the mine and although he'd suggested to the blonde at the store that he might be back, he'd promised Marie for sure that they could screw some more come sundown.

The lay of the land was new to him past Hanging Rock. But, as open as the slopes were, it seemed it would be hard to ambush folks along here. He came to Black Butte, where they dug coal for the railbed. He didn't stop. Nobody had stolen any coal, and he knew you never found metallic ores around coal mines.

By the time he got to Pipestone he was hungry and his mount was a mite jaded. He stopped in Pipestone to feed and rest them both. As Copper had some oats in the livery, Longarm had steak and eggs in the one open-air beanery. He ordered extra coffee. For some reason, he was feeling a little tired for this time of the day. He figured it was the altitude.

As he ate and jawed with the motherly old gal who served simple fare to all hungry comers, he got such gossip about mining conditions as Pipestone had to offer. There wasn't much. The mine was breaking better than even, but since they only dug poor to middling grade ore up here, they hadn't lost any horn silver or gold dust to the Timberliners.

He stopped for water up the line at Lost Hat. He knew the Bordon gals had relations there, but he didn't inquire about that. He knew that Livia, her kids, and likely anyone she knew well enough to sleep under the same roof with had to be sort of wicked. But he was looking for train robbers, not sex maniacs. He already had enough of *them* to worry about, and it was a good thing Livia and the kids were out of his hair.

The mine super at Lost Hat was a friendly, sensible cuss, but couldn't tell Longarm anything he didn't already know. Like the mines further down the line, they dug no horn or dust. So the only mine getting really victimized was the one at the end of the line, Triple Tits—or, to give it its post office address, Trinippy.

By either name, the folks up at the end of the line seemed mad as hell about it when Longarm finally rode in.

A couple of locals came up to Longarm as he was watering and rubbing down Copper in front of the one and only general store. They told him it was about time he'd arrived, as they'd heard the mighty Longarm was in the territory, but hadn't caught any of the Timberliners yet.

"Simmer down, boys," he said. "I only got two heads

and eight arms. I came up to talk about the robberies with your mine super."

One of the miners pointed at a shack under a conveyor incline up the slope. "You'll find her in there. She wants to talk to you, too."

Longarm started to ask what they meant, but they'd already said their super was a she. He'd heard some gals were attending the Colorado School of Mines lately. At the rate they were going, they'd start voting and smoking cigars any day now.

He made sure his mount was tethered comfortably and legged it up to the super's office shed. As he approached, a formidable-looking gal in a whipcord riding outfit opened the door and stood there, hands on hips, looking mean as hell.

He introduced himself and she said to call her Molly and come on in. The office was cluttered and untidy, but that figured. Old Molly was a mess, too.

She was almost as tall as Longarm and outweighed him by at least forty pounds. Her suntanned face was ugly and her hair was streaked with gray. He took the seat she offered, feeling better about her being a she-male. He hardly ever got in trouble with fat, ugly old gals. She looked tougher than half the men he'd ever met.

She talked tough, too. She dropped her big rump on a stool and demanded, "All right, Longarm. What are you doing about the motherfuckers who've been stealing my high grade?"

He laughed and, seeing it was to be man to man, replied, "I ain't after anyone for incest, Miss Molly. As to the Timberliners, I wouldn't have ridden all this way if I wasn't working on the case."

She snorted. "You're wasting time at the wrong end of the line. It's an inside job. It's the fucking railroad that's behind the so-called robberies. They ain't fooled me. I've never knowed a railroad as wasn't run by crooks. You know what I thinks, Longarm?"

153

"No, but I'm sure you'll tell me, ma'am."

"Don't call me ma'am. Jest call me Molly. Are them shoulders real, or is that coat padded?"

"You were going to tell me about the Timberliners, Molly."

"There ain't no Timberliners. It's them crooks running the narrow-gauge. They're jest pretending to get held up so's they can skim the cream off my ore. They already charges us an arm and a leg for taking it down the mountain. But the greedy sons of bitches wants it *all!*"

"That's a mighty serious charge, Molly. Have you any proof?"

"Sure. Elimination. I ain't stealing silver and gold. I doubt you're stealing silver and gold. So who's left? Nobody handles what we ships but us, the railroad, and mill. The mill ain't doing it. Cal Thayer, the assay man, is independent of both the mills and the narrow-gauge, and he keeps 'em straight by marking the bullion produced from each claim. Not one gold or silver brick has turned up missing between the mill and Denver. So the millhands must be so honest it's disgusting."

She stopped to get her breath before she went on at full steam. "I suspicioned the millhands and even old Cal Thayer at first. But they won't work as the crooks. The assay man only grades and keeps track of the produce. He never has more'n an ounce or so in his possession and, in any case, he don't sell bullion. Neither do any of the other merchants up or down the line. As to the millhands, if they was crooks who wanted to lay aside for their retirement years, they'd never mess around pretending to be train robbers. They wouldn't have to."

Longarm said, "I have been wondering about that. Why rob crude silver north of town, when once or twice a week a load of pure bullion is shipped from the mills to the main line, on a longer and less populated stretch of rail spur? But don't you see that that puts the railroad men right back where we started, Molly?"

She looked blank.

He went on, "If the railroad men were robbing their own trains, why would they do it the hard way? A load of bullion down in the Indian country south of Peacock could vanish just as easy and take a lot longer before anyone heard about it. I hear tell there's no easy way to pack crude silver north, east, or west by horse or mule. True?"

"Sure it's true. The posses have covered every cross-country way out of the vale, and damn near rode off a mess of cliffs doing so. I tell you the loot is leaving these parts by *rail!* It's too damned bulky to be going any other way!"

Longarm saw that they were talking in circles. So he asked if she was fixing to ship any horn or dust in the near future. She said she was and led him out and down the slope to the rail siding. A car of low grade was standing ready to roll. A sleepy-eyed but armed guard was hunkered down by half a dozen canvas sacks, smoking a pipe. Molly nodded to him and opened a sack for Longarm's inspection. He reached in and took out a fistful of horn silver to study.

Horn silver looked just like it was called. Like a busted-up cow horn, albeit with a silvery sheen. The flat flakes ranged in size from a dinner plate down to a fifty-cent piece. Molly explained that the plates were found in natural cracks in the lower grade ore body. At a time when the world was younger and hotter, water filled with silver salts had cooked dry in the cracks, leaving what amounted to almost pure silver, rusty with chlorine. He already knew you could boil the chlorine out of the silver, easy, to get pure bullion. But she told him again anyway. She said, "Any fool could reduce that horn on a pot-bellied stove, given a clay pot and a pinch of sodium silicate."

"Ain't that what they call water glass, Molly?"

"Damn right. You can buy it almost anywhere. Farmers use it to preserve eggs. Stir dry sodium silicate in a pot of molten horn silver and the chlorine garbs holt of the sodium to form common sodium chloride—table salt. The left-over silica is plain quartz. Both rises as a scum, leaving the pure bullion in the bottom of the pot. You could do her over a campfire."

He shook his head. "No, you couldn't. Nobody's seen any campfires in the hills around. If they're reducing it before fencing it, it must be indoors."

Before she could argue about that, they heard a toot. Longarm put the horn silver back in the sack and tied it tight before turning to watch the Shay from Peacock grunt on up the grade. He consulted his watch and saw that they'd be getting back to Peacock about five, going downhill a damned sight faster than he'd ridden up.

The Shay dropped its combination and steamed up to the end of the line, where it started to circle around to wind up pointed the right way. As they waited, a couple of Tom Carrol's railroad dicks got out of the one passenger coach and joined Molly and Longarm.

They introduced themselves as Phil and Alex. Phil was short and Alex was tall. They said they had a message for Longarm from their boss. The bullion he'd sent special had arrived that morning in Denver safe and sound, along with the man he'd shot it out with in the roundhouse. The special from Tolland had come back to Tolland just after Longarm had ridden out of Peacock, and all seemed right with the world.

Longarm said he'd get his horse and load it aboard the train. Phil said he was glad Longarm would be riding back with them, packing horn, and asked if he had any special orders.

Longarm said, "Yeah. I want you boys to ride atop the last car, with eyes peeled and chambers loaded. I'll be forward in the locomotive. If I start shooting at anything, you'd best shoot at her, too."

"That don't sound particularly ingenious, Longarm."

"I know. The Timberliners are simple folk, too. They've been using the same method, over and over again, on the same stretch of track. I reckon it's about time somebody called a halt to it."

The train rolled down past one camp after another, with Longarm standing behind the engineer, who doubtless knew

156

he meant it when he said to run her slow. They rattled past the coal mine at Black Butte, where some children waved at the train. Longarm waved back. He'd been a kid one time.

They passed through Hanging Rock. No flag was up, so they didn't stop. A skinny gal with ash-blond hair was standing on the platform looking wistful as she waved. Longarm waved at her, too. He figured he owed her that much.

The engineer said, "Well, it's a clear track on down to Peacock." "I know," Longarm said. "Slow down some more."

"Slow down? We're barely crawling, Longarm."

"Slow down to eight or ten miles an hour, anyway. Up to now, the Timberliners have never tried to board a moving train going any speed at all. I suspicion they might not have horses close enough to matter, since nobody's ever seen one, and it's mighty bleak out there."

The engineer shut the throttle and just let the Shay roll, holding her to ten miles an hour with the brakes. Longarm stood in the doorway, gazing up the barren, rocky slope with his Winchester across his chest. They rounded a slight bend and the engineer gasped, "Jesus!"

Longarm opened fire up the slope, and snapped, "Give her full throttle! Now!"

"There's a big boulder on the tracks ahead, Longarm!"

Longarm swore, reached past him, and opened the throttle wide as the engineer covered his face with his hands and cried, "I can't look! Goodbye, mama! Goodbye, kids!"

It looked spooky to Longarm, too, as the little engine picked up speed and bore down on the waist-high boulder blocking the roadbed. For one awful moment he wondered if he'd guessed wrong. Then the cow catcher hit the boulder and pitchforked it off the tracks to bound lightly down the slope to the dry creekbed to their left.

Longarm laughed as the train moved even faster. "Take this fool throttle," he told the engineer. "I can't do everything myself, damn it!"

157

The engineer uncovered his eyes in wonder as the fireman rose from the steel deck to marvel, "I don't believe it! We hit that big rock going lickety-split and we hardly even felt the bump!"

Longarm didn't answer. They'd rounded another curve and he was too busy leaning out the side, pumping and firing his Winchester at the two men coasting down the grade ahead of them in a rusty old ore tram from some mine or another. The high sides of the ore tram were sheet steel, but not thick enough to stop a .44-40 slug. So the owlhoot trying to man the brakewheel of the tram let go of it when Longarm gutshot him.

His partner managed to bounce a revolver slug off the steel jamb near Longarm's head. Then he was down, too. The tram came to another curve, running wild.

Longarm said, "Now you can hit the brakes."

The mine tram left the tracks to bound ass over teakettle down the slope, spilling its passengers like broken and discarded rag dolls as it did so. By the time the Shay slid to a stop, the tram and both bodies were small dots down among the boulders of the dry creek.

Longarm jumped down on the high side. As he started legging back the way they'd just come, cutting upslope at an angle, the two railroad dicks were climbing down and calling after him.

Longarm stopped and pointed. "Go down amongst the rocks and see if them rascals are anyone you might know," he told them.

"Where are *you* going, Longarm?"

"To see who I shot, of course," Longarm replied, moving on.

It took him some time to reach the first fake rock. He circled in, wary, and then lowered his muzzle as he saw that the man sprawled upslope behind it was alive—barely.

"Howdy," Longarm said to him. "I can see by the way you're gasping that you ain't long for this world, old son. Do you have any interesting last words to say?"

The owlhoot had been ventilated through the ribs. "Go

158

to hell," he groaned. "How did you figure it out?"

Longarm kicked the fake rock and it rolled downhill a
ways. "I studied the country some as I rode up the tracks
today," he said. "These rocks weren't here the last time I
passed. They're tolerable good, for staff covered with granite dust and shellacked. But once I started looking for rocks
big enough to hide behind, and kept track of the same, you
stuck out like sore thumbs. So, now that I've satisfied your
curiosity, how's about telling me who sent you boys up here
toting all this ingenious stage scenery?"

The man he'd shot right through a fake hollow rock
didn't answer. Longarm knelt, felt the side of his throat,
and muttered, "Shit. Might've known you were a sissy."

He searched for I.D., didn't find any, and moved on.
Behind the second fake rock he found a dead man spread-
eagled on his back. He was a handsome devil. But Longarm's round had gone right through his shirt pocket, scat-
tering tailor-made cigarettes all about like confetti. That was
all the I.D. the pretty boy carried, save for a waxed bus-
cadero gunrig that hinted at a misspent past.

The third and last body lay behind the third and last fake
rock. He was an older man with gray whiskers. He had
nothing in his pockets giving any name or address and
identifying him from old wants was going to be a chore,
with half his face blown off like that.

Longarm turned to head back to the train, leaving the
cleanup to the doubtless willing local lawmen from town.
As he approached the tracks, the taller railroad dick, Alex,
said, "Phil just yelt up the slope that the men you spilled
off the mountain are total strangers to him."

Longarm took out a smoke and lit it. "There seems to
be a lot of that going around. It appears these underlings
were just saddle tramps and no-goods, recruited for the job.
I know for a fact that a hired gun called McKane was coming
up here to work with 'em. The masterminds were too scared,
or too slick, to show themselves during the robberies."

"How in hell did you know all them rocks was paper or
something, Longarm?" Alex asked.

Longarm said, "Easy. If they'd been real rocks, nobody could have carried them about from job to job. I owe you boys an apology, now that I see how they flummoxed you. By shifting stage scenery, they set up their ambushes where you regular riders on the line wouldn't be expecting them. Bluffing a train to a halt, they just marched the crew and passengers out of sight, loaded the loot in that mine tram, and coasted off downhill. That's why none of the posses ever scouted hoof sign or any other when they rode out looking for the rascals."

Alex frowned. "I see up to a point. They sure as hell never rode that tram down the vale into Peacock. Somebody would have noticed."

"Sure. After robbing a train, they rode it to a safe distance, hid it on some siding, and likely drifted in to Peacock innocently, one at a time. In a mining town, nobody questions a strange face, unless he's biting somebody on the leg in the saloon. Once we get the bodies lined up for the folks in town to look over, I'm sure someone's sure to say they noticed one or more just spitting and whittling about town."

Alex nodded. "Sure, but what about that tram full of loot? There ain't no switch or siding this side of Peacock, Longarm. You can take my sworn word on that!"

"I do, Alex. You forget I just rode up this very same track, looking."

"Then how in hell did they ever leave the tracks with that tram? It might have been dinky next to yon locomotive, but it sure as hell wouldn't fit in a pocket worth a damn!"

Longarm sighed. "I'm still working on that. There were five of 'em just now. A few others might have got away, or been waiting someplace. Half a dozen men might be able to pick up and tote a mine tram a short way, if they put their minds to it."

"Full of stolen ore, Longarm?"

"Hell, Alex. The loot was loose, not nailed to the tram's bottom."

"Oh, I see. They unloaded the bags of high grade, hid 'em, and then picked up the tram to do the same. But no matter how you slices it, nobody could have had that tram hid far from the tracks, and we've gone over ever nook and cranny within miles of Peacock more'n once!"

"I said I was still working on it. Let's get us all aboard and see the passengers and such safe to town, Alex. I'm anxious to see who acts the most surprised when they learn in town that this time the Timberliners didn't get away with it."

Chapter 14

It didn't work. Everyone in Peacock seemed excited and surprised to hear that Longarm had foiled the latest holdup attempt by the mystery gang. If some people didn't share in the general enthusiasm, they were too slick to show it. Of course, only half the town came down to the station to celebrate.

Dave, the deputy who'd sort of taken the late Marshal Bordon's place, said he'd be proud to send a buckboard crew out to gather in the dead and the phony rocks as evidence. Longarm said he'd be much obliged, and added, "I got another chore for you, Dave. I know you're the local law here, now, but..."

"Hell, name it, Longarm! As far as I'm concerned, you just holler froggy and we'll jump!"

"That's mighty neighborly, Dave. All right. I want you to send a pair of deputies up to the Divide and gather in Scotty Gunn, sheep and all."

"You want that sissy kid arrested, Longarm?"

"Not hardly. I'm sending more than one because it's against Colorado law to leave a sheep herd untended in the mountains. It'll be dark long before they can get sheep and sheepherder down here, but there's a full moon tonight and Scotty has a tolerable sheepdog. Have your boys tell Scotty

I said it might be dangerous up there for the next few days, so I want all the sheeps and bo-peeps down here where I can keep an eye on 'em."

"You reckon some survivors might be headed over the pass, Longarm?"

"Anything's possible. I'll wire the law in Hot Sulphur Springs to keep an eye out on the far side of the Divide. I'll ask a ramrod I know to have his cowhands keep an eye on the trails headed east. We don't have the manpower to chase after them in every infernal direction. Meanwhile, Scotty's up there alone right now, Dave."

Dave said he'd take care of everything, so Longarm headed for the Western Union office. He picked up a couple of replies to earlier messages he'd sent and wrote Billy Vail a report on the latest developments, trying not to sound too boastful. As he came out of the Western Union, he saw the stage from Tolland roll in and stop across the street in front of a saloon. That sort of surprised him.

He was even more surprised when he saw Billy Vail and a gent in a funny outfit dismounting from the stage. The stranger was dressed like the late Prince Albert and had a flower in his buttonhole. As Longarm approached, the prissy-looking dude shook hands with Billy Vail and walked away. Vail saw Longarm at the same time and came to meet him, walking as fast as his stubby legs would carry him.

Longarm said, "Howdy, boss. I'm surprised to see you, twice. I didn't think the stage was running today, and I just sent you a wire addressed to the Denver office."

Vail grabbed Longarm by the arm. "Let's find a place where we can talk quiet. You're in a hell of a mess, son. I caught the first train out of Denver this morning but when I got off in Tolland the assholes tried to tell me the stage only ran on occasion, when they had a full load."

Longarm chuckled. "I see you had no trouble persuading them different. Let's go find a booth in the saloon while you tell me what brings you this way, all lathered up."

They went inside, grabbed a booth in the back, and told the waiter they wanted needle beer and no company. As soon as it was safe to talk, Vail told Longarm, "You just made a God-awful mistake, Longarm. You gunned a fellow lawman! It gets worse. He was federal!"

Longarm let some smoke trickle out his nostrils as he studied on the accusation. Then he nodded. "I get it. I thought I'd seen that face before, shaved and with its eyeballs more in place. I had to shoot him, Billy. He was out to shoot me."

"You wired me that, but you still screwed up, son. The man in the box you sent to Denver was the missing post office dick, Crawford."

The waiter came with their drinks. Longarm took a sip of suds. "That tastes good after a hard day's work. Don't you want to hear about what I just done, Billy?" he asked.

"Screw what you done today! I'm talking about last night! I knew as soon as I saw him in the Denver morgue that you'd blown the brains out of another federal officer! What in hell made you act so ornery, Longarm?"

Longarm took another sip of beer, put down the schooner, and said, "Well, as long as you're so infernally interested in less important side-shows, I'll start at the beginning. It's come back to me, just now, that I once worked on another case with Crawford, up near Cheyenne. I'd forgotten all about it. But it's easy to see Crawford didn't. He must have pulled something crooked when we were working on the same side. Something I missed, but he couldn't know that."

"Jesus, you mean he was gunning for a fellow federal officer, too?"

"It's sure starting to look like it, boss. He was up here working on the train robberies for the Post Office Department. Likely working on it honest and true, but not getting anyplace. I'll tell you in a minute how tricky the train robbers were. Naturally, Crawford heard I was coming up here to help out. At least, that's what they told him. But the man had a guilty conscience. He couldn't know for sure I wouldn't recall that other old case where he seemed to be screwing up, and he didn't want me raising any questions about his past performance. So the first move he made was to vanish his fool self. He let his whiskers grow and hid here abouts, pretending to be kidnapped or worse."

Vail sipped some suds of his own. "That wouldn't have worked for long, knowing how good you are at finding missing folks."

Longarm nodded. "He didn't aim to give me much chance to look for him. He duped Lynx and Spud, a pair of no-goods he might have had something on, into laying for me at the Tolland stop. Not knowing me on sight, they gunned the only man getting off who fit my description."

"Yeah. I've been meaning to ask why you went on to Salt Lake City."

"Like I said, diversionary tactics. To get back to Craw-ford and his dupes, they reported me dead, so he killed 'em, then rode back to the place he was staying for the moment. He was boarding with the late Marshal Bordon and some sassy gals I'd best not gossip about since I'm in no position to witness in court against them. Anyhow, just as Crawford had me down as dead, I showed up. Bordon went home and told him. Crawford must have shit his pants to hear I was still alive. But, thinking fast, he moved out sudden and they invited me to stay in his place. Partly to throw me off— and partly because the gals were naturally hospitable."

"Hold on. Are you saying Marshal Bordon was in with the crooks?"

"Not all of them. Just Crawford. He had no choice. Crawford had some family matters he knew about to black-mail Bordon with. It hadn't started out that way. Poor old Bordon was just hosting a fellow lawman more than the law allows, till Crawford got desperate and used it to blackmail him into helping. That's the trouble with staging wild orgies in the privacy of one's own home. They only work as long as nobody in the group turns mean. I don't think the gals were in on anything but slap and tickle. Two, at least, were too dumb to keep any family secrets, and Bordon could have done twenty at hard for what Crawford had on him. So once I was in town poking about, Crawford forced the marshal to back him and, together, they tried to ambush me. It didn't work. I put a pistol ball in Bordon instead."

Vail shook his head. "Hold on! I read what you wired. Marshal Bordon was gunned down on the trail to Tolland. You never done that, did you, Longarm?"

"Not hardly. After I winged Bordon and they run off into the night together, Bordon went home, likely feeling poorly, but pretending to be drunk as his wife—uh—distracted me some. Bordon couldn't go to a doctor here in Peacock, but the bullet I'd put in his liver wasn't going to fall out by itself. So, next day, he rode for other parts and medical attention by himself. Crawford knew that no matter where Bordon was treated for the gunshot, sooner or later I'd find out. So he joined Bordon on the trail, and as they talked friendly, slapped leather and killed him with a bullet of his own. See?"

"I do now. It fits. Two .44-40 rounds in the same body. How was anyone to know they came from different guns?"

"I missed it myself. You want the rest? All right. Having gunned his last ally, Crawford had to come for me on his own. He did—and he lost. So much for that loose end. Can I tell you about the train robbers now?"

Vail shook his head. "We're still missing one name. Who was the innocent bystander gunned down in your place at Tolland?"

"Oh, that's easy, Billy. An actor named Gaylord Jones was coming up here to be Macbeth in a play at the schoolhouse. According to a gal who once admired him, Jones and me was the same height and build. The reason he never showed up was that he got gunned in my place, poor cuss."

Billy Vail laughed out loud. "Hot damn! For once I caught you with your pants down, you self-confident rascal! Nobody never gunned Gaylord Jones. He just rode up from Tolland with me on the stage. He was obliged as hell about it, too. He'd been stuck down there waiting for the idjets to make a run, when I showed up and commandeered the coach. He even gave me his card and said if ever I wanted free tickets to a play he was appearing in, he'd remember the favor I done him. Want to see it?"

Longarm grimaced. "Not hardly. I might have knowed that gent getting down off the stage with you was an actor. Nobody else dresses like that."

He swallowed some beer to sort his thoughts as he studied on what Beth's—or Marie's old lover might mean. He'd told her he'd drop by the school later. It could wait. He knew it figured to be a messy scene, no matter how two acting folks played it.

Vail was grinning like a weasel in a henhouse across the table as he insisted, "Go on, smartass, tell me who they gunned by accident in your place!"

Longarm grinned back and said, "There's only one gent it could be, boss. It's too bad poor Crawford didn't know. He could have played hero instead of pussyfooting after me in that roundhouse. The man they gunned for me was Kandy McKane, the hired gun the train robbers had recruited from Dodge. Crawford and his hired dupes didn't know who they were gunning. So they didn't get to collect the reward they had coming. Ain't that a bitch?"

Vail started to object. Then he said grudgingly, "It works. We'll check it for sure, later. All right, the Post Office Department will likely buy your excuse for gunning one of their agents, after all. What else have you been up to, you crazy bastard?"

Longarm called the waiter over for more beer, then brought Vail up to date so far. When he got to where the unidentified bodies being due in town almost any time, now, Vail nodded. "You done good, son. I'm sorry I cussed you for shooting a postal inspector in the line of duty. Now that it's over, we'd best study on getting back home. They say the stage is running back to Tolland and the D&RG Western at six, and God knows when we'll ever have another chance to get out of here."

Longarm looked surprised. "You go on home if you want to, boss. I ain't half finished up here yet."

"Do tell? How come? You just blew away the whole gang—or most of it. Any survivors are moving at the moment fast and far. Let other lesser lights of the law worry about 'em. They sure as shit won't ever hold up another train in these parts!"

Longarm sipped some beer, nodded, and said, "Well, their method is mostly exposed. They'll play hell stopping trains with fake rocks again. But ain't you the least bit curious about the brains behind it all, Billy?"

"Sure I am, assuming they weren't in the head of that old-timer you blew them out of this afternoon. But, even assuming they had confederates telling them when the horn silver was coming down the mountain and such, you have to drop a case when it starts to bottom out, Longarm. It could take months to find out who might or might not have been a mite two-faced in these parts. Whoever they were, they ain't in business any more. You must have scared them out of a year's growth. They'll never show their hand to anyone now."

Longarm shrugged. "I know I might have made more honest men out of some, of late. But that ain't the point, Billy. The saddle bums I had it out with up the line weren't high enough on the totem pole to matter. Like the drifters Crawford used, they were just pawns."

"I ain't arguing about that, Longarm. I'm arguing about the time we have to waste on nitpicking when there's a world full of really dangerous crooks out there. Do you have the least notion who you're after now that you just smoked up their field workers?"

"Not yet, Billy. There's too many on my list."

"There you go. They still have county and town law here in Peacock. Tell them your suspicions and let them gnaw at the leftover bones."

"Can't, boss. Pete, Dave, and such likely mean well, but they're so dumb it's spooky. They've had all this time to catch the crooks, and you can see how well they done so. Look—if you want to hang about until I wrap it up, Tom Carrol can likely board you at his house up the slope."

"Where will you be bedding down, then?"

"Ain't sure. I had a place in mind, but it might be taken.

In any case, I may be up half the night."

"Doing what? You just said you didn't know who the masterminds were."

Longarm smiled thinly. "I told you I didn't know for sure who I was after. Not that I didn't have some notions on where to look. I'm just waiting for dark, and for things to quiet some, before I get back to work. What I have in mind is sort of sneaky."

Chapter 15

Longarm left his mount in the livery and headed up the grade on foot, with his Winchester in one hand and an unlit bull's-eye lantern in the other.

The moon was full, and so was the town behind him. The bodies propped up for public perusal in the window of Smiley's undertaking establishment had attracted folks from all up and down the line and, while nobody seemed to know for sure who the vaguely familiar drifters might be, the results had been good for the saloon trade. It hardly seemed likely anyone would miss one face in the crowd, even this early.

He was wrong. He heard familiar footsteps clumping up the ties behind him. So he stopped, turned, and said, "Evening, boss. I hope you brought serious hardware."

Billy Vail joined him, hefting a considerable twelve-gauge as he replied. "Borrowed this scatter gun from the boys at the jailhouse. How come you lit out without telling me, old son? Don't you work for me no more?"

"Hell, Billy, I figured you were busy. You were talking to old Tom Carrol and I figured . . ."

"Bullshit!" Vail snorted, adding, "It only took one hint to get Tom and his old woman to offer shelter for the night, and you knew it. You headed out alone because you got

170

something unconstitutional—and, most likely, wild and immoral—in mind."

Longarm sighed. "When you're right you're right, boss. Let's go on back to town and forget all about it."

As he'd hoped, Vail frowned and said, "Hold on now. I know I've chided you in the past about some of your rough-hewed methods, Longarm. But how close are we to some serious arresting and—uh—how unconstitutional do you reckon it might get?"

Longarm shrugged. "Don't know. That's why I like to work alone. Might have to do some breaking and entering without a search warrant."

"Oh, shit, is that all? I feared you were in one of your wilder moods, like the time you deputized that band of wild Injuns. I had one hell of a time explaining all those scalped outlaws to Washington. Lead on and I shall follow and fear no evil, for between us we must be the two meanest bastards in the valley."

Longarm laughed and led Vail up to the tunnel north of town. Inside the dark entrance, he struck a match and lit his bull's-eye.

Vail said, "I thought this tunnel had been checked out more'n once."

"So it has, *visual*," Longarm answered.

He stepped off the tracks and moved along the upslope wall, rapping gently on the jagged rock with the muzzle of his Winchester. Vail asked him what on earth he was looking for.

"Staff. That's what they call burlap covered with plaster and painted to look like most anything. Learned about it from the schoolmarm down at the far end of the railyards."

"You told me about the pet rocks that weighed about ten pounds each. Do you suspicion this schoolmarm of being in on all these scenic effects?"

"Hardly, Billy. For one thing, it would have been dumb as hell of her to start showing the whole drama club how to fake rocks and such if she was constructing scenery for the train robbers. For another thing, they tried to run a locomotive over her. The masterminds must have been mad enough to spit when a strange gal showed up and started giving lessons in plaster and paint. They knew it was only a question of time before someone like me put two and two together."

He stapped a slab of rock that looked suspicious, saw it was real, and moved on, adding, "There's at least one crook working as a railroad yardman. He can keep for now. But when this is all over, I'll find out from the dispatcher who was working the switches in the yard on the day they tried to kill Miss Simmons with a runaway train. They wouldn't have let her run if they hadn't been sure the tracks were open the right way."

The gun muzzle thunked against something hollow. "Here we are," Longarm said. "There must be a hinge and latch somewhere, but what the hell, it's flimsy stuff. Hold this lantern, will you?"

He gave Vail the bull's-eye and took out his jackknife. He stabbed the blade through what looked like solid granite. As Vail watched in wonder, Longarm simply carved out a man-sized doorway for them. He let the staff he'd cut loose fall free and took the bull's-eye back to step inside.

Vail followed. They found themselves in a low tunnel blasted through solid rock. The chief marshal whistled. "This must be an old mine drift. You can see it's cut too square to be natural."

Longarm said, "This wasn't part of the old Peacock copper mine. It was tunneled extra, after the railroaders drilled the tunnel back there. It would have been mapped by the railroad engineers if they'd drilled into a mine." He pointed the beam down at the solid but dusty floor and added, "See the silvery streaks? That's where they rolled the mine tram in to hide between holdups. After coasting downgrade and into the railroad tunnel, a dozen men could just pick her off the tracks and manhandle her in here out of sight. It'd be here, now, had not I sent it down into the dry creek."

They moved on and in less than fifty yards they came to a cross tunnel, much bigger, with the low roof above braced here and there by pit props of spruce. *"This* is part of the abandoned mine," Longarm said. "The masterminds knew it ran almost to the surface near that tunnel back there. So they just drilled through and hung that curtain of fake rock over the new and unknown exit. They made sure the main adit south of town was caved in, to keep kids and other curious folk out. But, naturally, they have to have another way in and out down in Peacock. Might have used an old vent, or just drilled through from some rascal's cellar. We'll find out directly."

He started down the considerable grade of the abandoned mine drift, moving slow and scanning all about with the beam of his lantern. Vail had been thinking. He said, "This tunnel wasn't supposed to run this way, according to the map that turned up in Thayer's files. That chart had all the drifts running deep to the west, caved in."

Longarm snorted in disgust. "You can see they only caved in the old drifts near the adit. The map was a fake. I knew that the minute I saw it. Somebody whipped it up special for my edification, Billy. It was drawn with diluted brown ink, then smeared with soil and folded a lot to look old. Likely by the same hands that fashioned all that fake rock."

"Well, I'll take your word for it, since even I can see that map had the layout all wrong. You sure have an eye for sign, old son."

"Hell, Billy, that map was smeared with *soil*. Old papers lying about an office file don't get smeared with garden dirt. They dust up with soot, fly specks, and spider shit. And you don't *fold* charts or blueprints. They're kept flat in a drawer or rolled in a pasteboard tube."

"By jimmies, you're right! It's no wonder Thayer was surprised he had the chart after all. Some tricky son of a bitch whipped it up when you started asking about the old mine and snuck it into the assay office files!"

"That's about the size of it. Keep your voice down. We're coming to a wide spot in the road."

They eased into an intersection of tunnels where, in the

past, the real honest copper miners had set up a work station with a workbench and some shelves. The old wood was covered with dust and bat droppings. But a big new coffee grinder stood bolted to the old workbench.

Vail murmured, "This is surely an odd place to grind coffee, don't you agree?"

Longarm nodded, shone the beam at the dirty floor below the spout of the heavy-duty coffee grinder, and said, "See those specks? They've been using this mill to grind the horn silver into fine grit. Turned to what looks to be sand, stolen horn could just sort of lay about in plain sight as mortar, chicken grits—damn near anything."

"Hot damn! So *that's* how they've been packing it out of the valley!"

"Not exactly, boss. Even a wagonload of building sand would attract some attention way the hell out on a country road. They've been mixing it with honest-dug ore and letting the honest-run foundry mills reduce the mix to bullion. Then they've been shipping the bullion, same as everyone else. Down to Denver via the D&RG Western, to sell openly on the market as legal, assay-stamped bullion."

He studied the floor, saw which way was layered with undisturbed dust, and took the other fork as Vail followed. Vail's voice was low but urgent as he said, "Damn it, Longarm, that won't work! We've been keeping tabs on the produce of all the mines on the line. Ain't one of them showed any unusual output since the robberies started. There's another reason it won't work. It's too damned complicated for the money involved. Save for the Triple Tits mine, all the produce coming down the mountain has been low to medium grade. The mines are barely busting even, with or without high grade being added to their produce. I don't know what the gents you shot this afternoon charged for their services, but the late Kandy McKane hired expensive. Add it up, Longarm."

"I did that right off, boss. I found it suspicious that such a big operation could be funded by the modest pickings of the train robberies, too. So I knew the masterminds already had some money. They needed rich but natural ore to high-grade a worthless mine they aimed to sell to a big syndicate at a real profit."

Vail trailed after him a ways, thinking, before he said, "Yeah, that works, if we knew which mine up the line we was talking about."

"It's the one at Hanging Rock," Longarm said. "It struck me odd right off that a half-ass silver mine was set between exhausted copper country and *coal beds*. All the other mines are lined up on the same formation, which gets richer as you go north. The Hanging Rock orphan was likely just an old try hole drilled by the copper company, then claimed as a silver mine by some slickers who hired innocents to widen and dig her serious. They're digging worthless country rock, but they don't know it. The so-called ore gets enriched down here, with sacks of what looks like sand, as the ore cars sit untended in the yards in the wee hours. The cars works their way into the honest-run mills, the salted ore gets ground up and reduced, and the results are ingots of silver with a proper bill of sale. Lately they've been hitting the market impured with just enough gold to whet the appetites of big, sneaky syndicate men who might see the advantages of buying a hole in the ground that only produces modest. In other words, the Hanging Rock mine's been shipping the cream of the Triple Tits mine."

"Can you prove this sort of wild notion, Longarm?" Vail asked. Longarm said, "Sure I can. I used my balls. Balls of tinfoil that belonged originally to a sort of odd woman-child, at any rate. When I visited the Hanging Rock mine I put a couple of fair-sized balls of tinfoil in their next ore shipment, covered with dirt and spit to look like rock, of course. This afternoon I got a wire from the Denver assay office, answering one I sent them. The few ingots of silver stamped as produce of the Hanging Rock Company had tiny traces of tin as well as stolen gold dust in 'em. Do I have to tell you there ain't an ounce of tin ore in the entire Rocky Mountains, Billy?"

"Nope. That ought to hold up in court, too. So who's

175

the major stockholder in the fake mine he wants to sell?"

"Keep your voice down, follow me, and we'll likely find out the less complex way. I sent out wires about that. But you know how Wall Street is. Takes them scribbly dudes a week to sharpen a pencil. Anyone sneaky enough to make boulders out of staff would likely have a smokescreen of fake names and holding companies to sort through in any case."

They trudged down the slope a spell, and Longarm judged they must be under Peacock, or damned near, when the beam of his bull's-eye flashed on what seemed to be a brick wall dead-ending the tunnel. He whispered, "I reckon this is about it, Billy. Have you got a round in your chamber?"

"Hell, no, I figured to *spit* at anybody I pointed this scattergun at. How are we going to get through that brick wall? It looks solid."

Longarm commenced to carve his way through with his knife.

On the far side of the fake cellar wall they found themselves, of course, in somebody's cellar. There were boxes, barrels, and bales all about. Longarm shone the beam on a flight of wooden steps, cautioned Billy to silence, and headed that way.

There was light coming under the crack of the door at the top of the stairs. So Longarm extinguished the lantern and set it down before easing up the treads on the balls of his feet, his Winchester muzzle trained on the doorway.

When he got to the top he heard voices, so he stopped just outside the door. Vail joined him silently. Old Billy was getting on in years and putting on lard from riding an office chair, but he was an old Texas Ranger and he knew when to shut up if he had to. Longarm cautiously tried the door knob as, on the other side of the panels, a voice whined, "I tell you we have to light out, damn it! The law has put half the gang out of action and it's only a question of time afore that fucking Longarm comes busting in on us!"

A more familiar voice replied, "Now, simmer down,

damn it. In the first place, running for it now would just make the bastards suspicious. In the second place, there's nothing linking us to them saddle tramps we hired to do our field work. So all we have to do is lay low till the heat dies down some. They don't know what we was really up to, boys. In a month or so we can start all over with a change of methods."

Longarm nudged his boss and whispered, "This door's locked from the far side. Have you heard enough?"

"I have," Vail said. "There are times for search warrants and there are times for common sense. Together?"

"Right—on the count of three."

They counted to three and hit the door with their combined considerable weight, and burst it wide open on the first try.

As the two lawmen crashed into the back room of Al Wrenn's hardware store, Longarm wasn't nearly so surprised as the boys in the back room were. But there were eight of them and as Longarm yelled "Freeze and grab sky!" everybody went for their guns at once.

Wrenn already had a shotgun cradled in his arms, so Longarm blew his face off first. Billy Vail gave a Texas yell and fired his twelve-gauge point-blank into old Smiley, the friendly undertaker. The local ticket agent for the casual stage line managed to get his S&W out, but flew back over the pot-bellied stove with Longarm's round in his head before he could fire. Billy Vail's awesome scatter gun did most of the damage as he pumped the small room full of shotgun pellets and billowing smoke. It got so bad that Longarm had to yell, "Hold your fire a minute, boss. I can't see anybody to shoot, if there is anybody."

There wasn't. As the lawmen waited, braced for anything, the smoke thinned to where they could make each other out. Nobody else was on his feet.

Vail kicked a body near his boots and said, "This one's done. I'd say we done 'em all, wouldn't you?"

As the haze thinned some more, Longarm looked around and said, "When you're right you're right. Let's go out and get some air. You surely stink up a place, Billy."

By the time they got out to the front of the closed store, folks who'd heard the shootout were pounding to be let in. Longarm opened the door for Dave the deputy, and old Tom Carrol.

"You're a mite late, boys," he said. "You'll find what's left of the Timberliners in the back room. Al Wrenn and Smiley were the ringleaders. Marshal Vail here can fill you in on the details. I still have a few chores to do."

As he stepped out onto the walk, Vail called out, "Hold on! Where the hell are you going now? I thought we just shot all the sons of bitches!"

Longarm said, "We may have. I'm—uh—sort of making me a social call, Billy. Why don't you fill the boys in, here, and I'll meet you all in the saloon in a few minutes."

Vail grinned. He'd forgotten that Longarm had mentioned a pretty schoolmarm.

Chapter 16

But that wasn't where Longarm was headed just yet. It was early. Beth/Marie would wait for him at the schoolhouse, if she aimed to. He meant to give her time to sort things out with that actor dude before he went anywhere near her. Meanwhile, he'd sort of lied to Billy Vail.

Billy was trigger-happy—considering how often he chewed Longarm out for gunning suspects—and it might be nice to bring in at least one member of the gang alive.

He got to the door of Calvin Thayer's assay office. It was locked. The light was off inside. That didn't mean nobody was there. He picked the lock with his jackknife's extra blade filed down to a skeleton key and went in. It only took a moment to confirm that the assayer had left for the night.

Longarm shrugged, went out again, and turned upslope at the next corner. He knew where Thayer lived alone. He hadn't been in the back room during the shootout, or in the crowd out front. Where else was left?

The side street was steeper going up than coming down from the Bordon house above Thayer's small frame cottage. The moon made up for the lack of street lamps, but everything was moonlit silver or inky black as Longarm followed the muzzle of his Winchester up the hill. A whitewashed board fence formed a corner ahead. Thayer's house was half a block above it. Longarm eyed the natural ambush warily as he approached, but saw no way of getting higher on the hill without risking it.

As he got almost within pistol range of the corner, he heard a gun go off. He crabbed sideways across the dusty street and dropped to one knee, looking for something to shoot back at even before it sunk in that the shot he'd heard hadn't been aimed at him.

A small, dark figure came into view from behind the whitewashed fence, holding a rifle aimed down at the ground. Longarm snapped, "Freeze!" A high pitched voice answered, "Is that you, Deputy Long? I thought it was when I shot the brute!"

Longarm rose and walked up to join Scotty Gunn as she pointed back the way she'd come. "He was aiming his pistol at you as I came down the slope behind him. Who on earth is he?"

Longarm walked over to the dark form lying face down in the weeds behind the fence and knelt to feel the side of his neck before he answered. "He used to be a crook named Thayer. I reckon he knew I'd be coming to ask him some questions. How did you get here so early, Scotty? What happened to your sheep?"

"I came on ahead to get away from those fresh-mouthed men you sent. They're herding my sheep down with Tinkerdog's help. They sure talked dirty all the way down the mountain."

Longarm said, "Well, they meant no harm. Nobody but me knows you're really a gal. We'd best get on down to the main drag and send a buckboard up for this dead rascal. Come on. As long as you insist on wearing pants, I'll buy you a drink while you meet my boss, Marshal Vail."

Scotty said she was willing, so they started down together. She asked him to tell her some more about the man she'd just shot in the back to save him.

"He was in cahoots with the crooks who were robbing trains and trying to slicker the mining interests in Denver with a worthless hole," Longarm said. "The details are tedious. What I had on him was that I caught him in some lies. I'm paid to do that, you see. He acted mighty innocent and helpful, but I'd played a sneaky trick with some bullion he said he was running an assay on. I knew he was just going through the motions when he failed to detect the tin I planted in the Colorado silver. He didn't think he really had to take the trouble to assay it, since he'd already helped the crooks to produce it. He knew to a grain how much gold they'd added as icing on the cake."

"Oh, so that's why he was crouched behind that fence waiting for you with a gun!" Scotty said.

"Yeah. Old Cal was educated better than most crooks. The hell of it was, I really didn't have anything I could prove on him in court, if he just hung tough and brazened it out. It's no crime to make a few mistakes. A jury might have got confused enough to let him off. Lucky for me, he panicked at a time I had a galfriend coming down the mountain unexpected. And, by the way, you know the cigarette butts you saw up the trail before, Scotty? I found their smoker today. He was still carrying them, crouched behind a fake rock that didn't stop bullets worth a hang."

Scotty snapped, "Those deputies told me about all that. And I never said I wanted to be your galfriend, damn it!"

"I was just speaking friendly. You surely can't be my boyfriend."

"Well, don't get any ideas. I'll belly up to the bar with you. But that's the only place you'll have my belly, if I have anything to say about it!"

He said it was her belly and she could rub it against anything she wanted to as far as he cared. He didn't tell her he already had a prettier gal by far lined up for later. It wouldn't have been polite, and he still wasn't sure.

They got down to the main street and, sure enough, Billy Vail was holding court in the saloon with half the town and all the law. The latest pile of dead had been added to the ones he'd gunned earlier, all wrapped in canvas and aboard a boxcar for delivery.

Vail was standing with his back to the bar, near the middle, with townies, railroaders, and lawmen all about. Longarm took Scotty's rifle and handed it across the bar with his own Winchester for safekeeping as he introduced her to Vail, not mentioning her gender. He saw the friendly yardman who'd thrown the lantern the night he'd had the shootout with Crawford and Bordon, so he called him closer and, as the yardman reached to shake, Longarm snapped the cuffs from his gunbelt around his wrist.

"You're under arrest," he said. "Would one of you railroad dicks grab hold of the other end of this?"

Alex took charge of the prisoner, but asked, "What's he charged with, Longarm?"

Longarm said, "Attempted murder. He was on duty when that runaway locomotive was aimed at the schoolhouse. They'd have never aimed her down the hill had they not been sure he was on the switches, to make sure it followed the right spur across the yards. Put him in the jail for now and I'll explain it all to his lawyer later."

As the prisoner was led out amid considerable jeers and comments on his mother's morals, Longarm told Vail and Dave about Thayer. Dave said he'd clean up the mess after he had a few more drinks.

Vail said, "I might have known you were up to something. Can one assume the case is finally wrapped at last? It's been a long day, and I'm getting sleepy."

"I want to go to bed, too. Do you have your own cuffs handy, Billy?" Longarm asked.

Vail unsnapped the cuffs from the belt under his coat, but looked about uncertainly as he handed them to Longarm. "I hope you don't have somebody left to arrest, old son."

Longarm's voice was sad as he replied, "I fear I do, boss, and it sort of hurts. Hold out your hands, Scotty Gunn. You are under arrest for impersonating a sheepherder, and other crimes too numerous to mention!"

Scotty did no such thing, of course, but she was hemmed in on all sides without her rifle. So it only took Longarm a few moments to subdue her and pin her against the bar with the cuffs on.

Vail stared down at her in wonder. "What did you say this little cuss done, Longarm?"

Longarm said, "She ain't a cuss, she's a gal as tells whoppers. She's been up on the Divide acting as a lookout for the Timberliners, and as part-time lover for a good-looking bandit who smokes sissy cigarettes!"

Scotty's eyes were glaring at him like a trapped wolf, but her voice was sweet reason as she pleaded, "You can't mean that, Longarm! I never lied to you once, I swear!"

Longarm looked at Vail. "There she goes, doing it again." Then he stared morosely down at the handcuffed girl in pants. "I'll spell it out for you so's you won't waste time telling lies to the jury, Scotty. When I told you I was looking for a jasper smoking cigarettes, you tried to throw me off with a wild yarn about his setting by the trail, smoking up a storm. I stopped by that rock you mentioned on the way down. It don't work, for two reasons. The view of the town is swell. But town is all you can see from that red herring place. Whilst *you* could see and doubtless signal the whole vale and the blind side of the Divide from up there in your lookout saddle." He grimaced and went on, "In the second place, the gang member we were talking about had no reason to be scouting for the others. He was a low man on the totem pole, even though you might have admired his totem pole some. This ain't delicate to mention in mixed company, but you was up there alone a lot, reading dirty books, too old to be the shy virgin you pretended—and, damn it, you never admired *me* at all! In all modesty, I've noticed that horny gals seldom pass up golden opportunities unless they already *have* somebody they sleeps with fairly regular."

"How do you know I wouldn't have given in to you? You never really tried. And, damnit, I just saved your life!"

"No, you never, Scotty. You gunned Thayer, no doubt to his considerable surprise, because the two of you were the last members of the gang and he likely told you he was afraid I suspicioned him. As to whether I might or might not have made a pass at a sheepherder, answer me this. You said you and your brother were tending separate herds for a widowed mother in Ward."

"It's true. I swear it!"

"You can swear all you like. But what brother, knowing how cowhands feel about sheepherders, is about to let his sister, even wearing pants, tend a herd so far from home, while he takes *his* sheep just a few miles from Ward?"

Vail said, "I reckon he's got you, miss. They do say confession is good for the soul."

Scotty Gunn snarled, "Oh, you can all just fuck yourselves!"

As they led the snarling bo-peep out, Vail asked Longarm, "Can I go to bed now?"

Longarm laughed. "Yep. That's where I aim to go, Lord willing and the creeks don't rise. We got it wrapped. I'll meet you in the morning for breakfast before you head back to Denver."

"Before *I* head back to Denver, Longarm? Where do *you* expect to be in the next few days?"

"Oh, I got to ship old Copper back to Salt Lake City. And wrap up a few other private matters, boss."

"Damn it, old son, do you mean to dally with some she-male on my time?"

"Don't know, Billy. I'm going to find out now."

It was later than he'd intended to call on his actress friend, but as Longarm approached the schoolhouse he saw that a light was still on inside. He grinned and walked faster. After all the excitement he'd had of late, he'd sort of forgotten how good old Beth/Marie made love. By the time he got to the door and opened it, his privates were tingling in anticipation.

But when he got inside, the actress wasn't there. One of her three witches was pushing a broom instead of riding it. She brightened when she saw Longarm. She said, "The other ladies ran home when they heard gunshots a while ago. I figured it was just some drunken hands letting off steam. So I stayed to clean up this mess. Someone has to. We threw the scenery we're not going to use out, but look at all this plaster dust and lint!"

Longarm frowned. "Can I assume the play is off, ma'am?"

"You can," the witch answered. "You can call me Lilly, by the way. We met the other day, when I was boiling and bubbling with my other weird sisters."

"I remember you, Miss Lilly. No offense, but you look better with your hair combed right. What happened to your acting coach? Or was it *two* acting coaches?"

Lilly leaned her broom against a school desk. "You mean you haven't heard? Beth Simmons left on the stage with that Gaylord Jones. That's why we had to cancel the play. It seems her Gaylord has a part in a play back in Kansas. He asked her to be his leading lady, and proposed marriage as well. That's enough cleaning for now. Oh, I nearly forgot. She left me this note to give you if you came by this evening."

Longarm took the small, sealed, scented envelope and put it in his pocket. He sighed and said, "I reckon they missed one another more than they'd expected. I'm happy for them both. She was a nice gal, and he seemed like a friendly enough gent, from the little I saw of him earlier."

Lilly said, "He was ever so gallant-talking and polite when he told us why the play had to be put off. Don't you mean to read the note—ah—Custis?"

"Later, maybe. I know what's in it. If it's any comfort to you witches, the play would have been postponed in any case. Your Macduff and Malcolm can't make it."

"Really? I want to hear all about it. Have you had supper yet?"

He had, but he wasn't stupid. "The tedious tale might be better told over coffee and cake, Miss Lilly. You—ah—live around here?"

She dimpled and said, "Just up the hill—alone. I'm a

widow woman. I run the notions store in town."

"I see. How's business been of late, Lilly?"

"Mighty slow. That's why I joined the drama club. I was hoping to add a little spice to my dull life and maybe get a chance to meet some people. But all I've gotten out of my life on the wicked stage, up to now, has been mighty dusty work."

She dimpled. "But why are we talking about it here? Let's just go up to my place, and while you put some logs on the fire I'll freshen up and we'll have all night to talk." She blushed and added, "I mean, that is, until you want to leave."

He knew what she meant. So he said he'd be proud to shove a log in her fireplace and she took his arm to lead him to his doom. She looked better outside, in the dark. As they walked arm and arm up the hill in the moonlight, he consoled himself that it could have turned out worse. After all, old Lilly was the witch with the nicest ass.

Watch for

LONGARM AND THE BUCKSKIN ROGUE

fifty-third novel in the bold
LONGARM series from Jove

Coming in March!